PUFFIN BOOKS

THE TELEVISION ADVENTURES OF MR MAJEIKA

Mr Majeika is no ordinary teacher. In fact, he is quite extra-ordinary, as Thomas and Melanie – and horrible Hamish Bigmore – soon discover.

Mr Majeika is a wizard from Walpurgis, and he has been sent to Britland to teach Class Three at St Barty's School. He tries very hard to behave, but from time to time a little bit of magic is called for. Hilarious and surprising events soon become daily occurrences at St Barty's.

Humphrey Carpenter is the author of three Mr Majeika books which inspired the television series, *Mr Majeika* and *Mr Majeika and the Music Teacher*, both published in paperback by Puffin, and *Mr Majeika and the Haunted Hotel*, published in hardback by Viking Kestrel. He has also written many books for adults and is co-author with his wife, Mari Prichard, of *The Oxford Companion to Children's Literature*. He lives in Oxford and has two children.

HUMPHREY CARPENTER

THE TELEVISION ADVENTURES

—— OF ——

MR MAJEIKA

Based on scripts by Jenny McDade
for the TVS production 'Mr Majeika'

PUFFIN BOOKS

PUFFIN BOOKS

Published by the Penguin Group
27 Wrights Lane, London W8 5TZ, England
Viking Penguin Inc., 40 West 23rd Street, New York, New York 10010, USA
Penguin Books Australia Ltd, Ringwood, Victoria, Australia
Penguin Books Canada Ltd, 2801 John Street, Markham, Ontario, Canada L3R 1B4
Penguin Books (N Z) Ltd, 182–190 Wairau Road, Auckland 10, New Zealand

Penguin Books Ltd, Registered Offices: Harmondsworth, Middlesex, England

First published 1988

Made and printed in Great Britain by
Richard Clay Ltd, Bungay, Suffolk
Filmset in 10½pt on 12pt Monophoto Baskerville

CONTENTS

Dedicated to Claire Sawyer,
Andrew Read, and Simeon Pearl
— Melanie, Thomas and Hamish
in the TVS production

1

HE'S MAGICAL, MELANIE!

'Seventy-nine!' said Mr Dudley Potter to himself, in a voice of the deepest gloom. 'Seventy-nine!'

Mr Dudley Potter was the headmaster of St Barty's School, in the sleepy English village of Much Barty. The sort of school where you'd expect everything to go along nice and quietly, with no trouble. Yet seventy-nine teachers had replied to Mr Potter's advertisement for someone to take Class Three at St Barty's, seventy-nine teachers had come to see St Barty's School, and when all seventy-nine of them had seen Class Three, they had said, 'No thank you,' and gone away again.

There was nothing wrong with Class Three itself. All – well, nearly all – the children in it were frightfully nice sensible children, like Melanie Brace-Girdle and her friend Thomas Grey, and plenty of others of the same sort. No, there was only one problem with Class Three. And that problem was Hamish Bigmore.

The last teacher of Class Three had been Miss Flavia Jelley. After a few terms of trying to teach Hamish Bigmore, Miss Flavia Jelley had been reduced to just that – a jelly. Finally Mr Potter had had to put Miss Jelley in a Home for Distressed School Teachers. She just couldn't cope with Hamish Bigmore. She said the sight of him made her scream.

The seventy-nine teachers who came to look at Class Three said the sight of Hamish Bigmore made them want to scream, too. That was why, at the beginning of the new term, Mr Potter found that he had nobody to teach Class Three. He was going to have to teach them himself.

From the drawer of his desk he took a large bottle marked Nerve Pills, and swallowed a handful. Desperately, he looked at his watch. Only an hour till school started. If only a new teacher could pop up from nowhere – could drop from the sky, as if by magic, and take Class Three for him – then everything would be all right. But magic didn't happen in a place like Much Barty.

'Failed again, Majeika,' said the Worshipful Wizard of Walpurgis.

The funny-looking chap in a wizard's hat and black robe stared miserably at the Worshipful Wizard through his big glasses. He looked a bit like an owl that had lost its way and blundered into a tree. 'Again, sir? Oh dear, oh dear.'

Apprentice Wizard Majeika of the Third Class Removed had been sitting his 'O'-Level Sorcery exams ever since he had been old enough to take them, at the age of ninety-five, which is the youngest age at which one may become a qualified wizard in the land of Walpurgis, where all the wizards come from.

'Yes, failed again, Majeika,' said the Worshipful Wizard. 'We're all very disappointed in you. Aren't we?' He looked at his fellow wizards, as they all sat at their high table under a ceiling of twinkling stars.

Nobody answered. Some of them looked as if they were thinking deeply, but if you peered closely you would have seen that they were snoring into their long beards. Spiders had spun cobwebs over several of them, and in the open mouth of one old sorcerer a mouse had made her nest and was bringing up a family of children.

Mr Majeika blinked sadly at the Worshipful Wizard. 'P-please, sir, can I try again?'

The Worshipful Wizard shook his head sadly. 'There has to be a limit to everything, Majeika. After all, this is the seventeenth time you've failed.'

'Yes, sir. I know, sir. But p-please . . .'

'This time, Majeika, you did worse than ever. All those silly spells! During the Spells Practical paper, Majeika, you sent sandcastles to the Sahara Desert, puppy dogs to Barking, and towels to Bath!'

'A-anyone can make a mistake, sir,' said Mr Majeika pathetically.

'But then, Majeika, there was the very sad case of your Aunt Betty.'

'Oh, *that*, sir! P-please don't mention that.' Mr Majeika began to sniff miserably.

The wizard with the mouse's nest in his mouth actually woke up and began to take notice; the mouse nervously gathered up her children and decided to find a home in another wizard's shoe, which had fallen off.

'You were supposed, according to the examination requirements,' said the Worshipful Wizard solemnly, 'to turn your Aunt Betty into a Bird of Paradise, weren't you, Majeika?'

'Yes, sir,' said Mr Majeika miserably.

'And instead, you turned her into –'

'A pheasant, sir.'

'And then what happened, Majeika?'

'She got shot down over Sandringham, sir.'

'And then?'

Mr Majeika's lip trembled. 'Sh – w-was served up as Christmas dinner, sir.'

(The pheasant had caused quite a sensation at the royal

9

dinner table, not least because it was wearing a tiny pair of high-heeled shoes.)

'Poor Auntie Betty,' muttered Mr Majeika, dabbing his eyes.

'In short, Majeika,' continued the Worshipful Wizard, 'you are a failure! There is not one spell, not one spot of Wizardry, that you've ever got entirely right.'

The wizard with the mouse's nest in his mouth shut his eyes again, and the mouse decided that the family might as well stay there for the time being. She tucked her children back in bed.

'I know, sir,' said Mr Majeika desperately. 'But I'm still young, sir. Well, relatively young, sir, only a hundred and forty-two, sir. If you'd just give me another chance, sir . . .'

The Worshipful Wizard smiled, though it was not a very kindly smile. 'I *am* giving you a chance, Majeika.'

'Oh, sir! Thank you, sir!'

'Though it's not, perhaps, the kind of chance you had in mind. Do you know, Majeika, what happens to wizards who fail their exams as many times as you have, Majeika?'

'Er, no, sir, I don't, sir.'

'They become,' said the Worshipful Wizard, pausing for dramatic effect, 'they become – *teachers*.'

'Teachers, s-sir?'

'Yes, Majeika, teachers!' The Worshipful Wizard gave a wave of his wand, and Mr Majeika's wizard hat flew off his head. Deprived of his Wizardship, Mr Majeika looked even more dazed and forlorn. 'A t-teacher, sir? Oh, no, sir! Anything but that, sir.'

But the Worshipful Wizard paid no heed. Again, he pointed his wand, and this time, with a click, a trapdoor opened in the floor in front of Mr Majeika. Far below could be seen a green and pleasant countryside.

'Down there, Majeika,' said the Worshipful Wizard, 'is the country of Britland, where we send our failed wizards. We send them there to become teachers. In Britland they languish, unloved, forgotten, and un-remarked upon. Never again to wizard!'

'Never? But sir . . .'

The Worshipful Wizard gave him no chance to finish his sentence. Raising his wand, he pointed it again, and poor Mr Majeika fell forward and tumbled through the trapdoor.

His cloak acted as a parachute, so that after the first tumble he fell quite gently. But it made him awfully giddy, and he opened and shut his mouth like a desperate fish as the countryside of Britland got closer and closer.

Thump! There he was, not too bruised, in the middle of a field. Around him, birds sang, and clouds scudded to and fro. In the distance a farmer was ploughing with a tractor. It was all very different from the magical, mysterious land of Walpurgis. Mr Majeika sighed, and scratched his head. A teacher! How did you become a teacher? Sitting in the middle of the field, he couldn't see anyone who needed teaching. Perhaps there had been a mistake, and he would be allowed to go back to Walpurgis and sit his exams all over again.

Bump! Mr Majeika's heart missed a beat. Something enormous had whizzed through the sky and crashed down beside him. It was big and black and rather old-looking, and it had three wheels. There was a label on it: 'Tricycle, Britland model, for the use of failed wizards who are to become Teachers.'

The tricycle had a box between the two back wheels, and tied to this was a broomstick. So perhaps he would be allowed to do some magic after all?

'No, Majeika,' boomed a voice. 'No magic.'

Mr Majeika blinked, and looked around. He couldn't see the Worshipful Wizard, but he could certainly hear him.

'No magic, sir?'

11

'*Nothing Walpurgian, Majeika. The broomstick is for emergency use only.*'

Mr Majeika sighed. 'Just as you say, sir.'

'*Now, Majeika, you will find a Book of Instructions in the box. And good luck, Majeika.*'

'Thank you, sir.'

Mr Majeika opened the tricycle box and found a small book entitled *Instructions for Walpurgians in the Country of the Britlanders*. The first instruction was: 'Travel by tricycle to the nearest habitation.'

Mr Majeika looked around him. At the edge of the cornfield was a road, and a signpost which said: 'To MUCH BARTY, 1½.'

One-and-a-half what? wondered Mr Majeika. And how did you travel by tricycle? He dragged the tricycle to the edge of the field and pushed it through the gate on to the road. Then he had a good look at it.

First he tried sitting on the handlebars, in the hope that the machine would carry him along magically. But of course things like that didn't happen in Britland. He tried running, in the hope that the trike would follow him. It didn't. He gave up, and sadly began to push it down the road.

Police Constable Bobby, the Much Barty policeman, was out for a training session with his dog, Trigger. P.C. Bobby wanted to teach Trigger to catch burglars, but Trigger wouldn't even run after sticks. He just lay on his back and kicked his legs in the air, hoping to be tickled. P.C. Bobby gave up, got on his bike, and began to pedal back to Much Barty, leaving Trigger to trot after him. He rather hoped the dog would get lost and find some other owner. As a police dog he was completely useless.

Rounding a bend in the road, P.C. Bobby was astonished to see a peculiar-looking chap with hair like a dish-mop and big round spectacles – not to mention a rather odd jacket and trousers – doing his best to push a big black tricycle. 'Got a flat tyre, have you?' called out P.C. Bobby. But the odd-looking person only blinked and stared. P.C. Bobby decided to make a note of the incident. Couldn't have any odd-looking fellows just wandering into Much Barty without some record being made of the fact. A respectable village like Much Barty wasn't the place for the likes of that character.

He got off his bike, licked his pencil, and thought for a bit. Then he wrote in his notebook: 'Saw a chap with a trike.' It didn't look quite right, not the sort of thing you put in a police report, thought P.C. Bobby, but he couldn't think what else to write.

Trigger caught up with him and lay down and kicked his legs up in the air.

'Stupid dog,' muttered P.C. Bobby, and pedalled off in disgust.

Mr Majeika stared after the policeman. So there *was* magic in Britland after all! A man balancing on two wheels! It was one of the most remarkable things Mr Majeika had ever seen. No one in Walpurgis could possibly manage something so clever.

He looked again at his trike. *It* had three wheels, but maybe . . . He climbed on to the saddle, and cautiously tried the pedals. Yes, it worked! Golly, how marvellous.

Pedalling unsteadily, he advanced towards the village of Much Barty. Suddenly he remembered that he hadn't looked at the rest of the instructions in his book.

'Britlanders ride on the left of the road, French on the right.' Mr Majeika puzzled over this. There was a white

13

line down the middle of the road. He decided to hedge his bets and stick to this.

There was another instruction in the book: 'On approaching settlements, reassure the inhabitants of your friendly intentions.'

Mr Majeika thought about this. How to show people he was friendly? The best idea seemed to be to sing a song.

Councillor Mrs Bunty Brace-Girdle, who considered herself to be the most important person in Much Barty, was doing some hurried shopping before dropping her daughter Melanie off at school. Mrs Brace-Girdle had summoned a meeting of the Keep The Village Pavements Tidy Committee for nine o'clock, and she wanted to get the shopping done beforehand.

She and her friend Mrs Sherwood-Greene met in the butcher's shop, and were deep in conversation about the agenda for the committee meeting. Melanie was bored; she wanted to get to school and see all her friends again. Also, she was wondering who would teach Class Three now that Miss Jelley had been put in a home.

Suddenly there was a peculiar noise, a kind of honking and shrieking all mixed together. Councillor Mrs Brace-Girdle and her friend Mrs Sherwood-Greene looked at each other in puzzlement.

Around the bend of the village street came a curious procession. First was a very odd man, in strange clothes, wearing big spectacles and riding a big black tricycle with a broomstick tied to the back. He was singing at the top of his voice:

> '*Now is the merry month of May,*
> *Tra-la la la la,*
> *Greensleeves is my delight,*
> *Tra-la!*'

14

He was riding the tricycle carefully along the white line in the middle of the road; behind him, honking their horns furiously, were all the cars, lorries and buses that couldn't get past.

'Good heavens!' said Mrs Sherwood-Greene. 'A tramp! A singing tramp in Much Barty!'

Councillor Mrs Brace-Girdle stared in amazement. 'How very eccentric. But are you sure he's a tramp, Dilys?'

'Well, Bunty dear, he certainly isn't a member of the golf club.'

The honking procession slowly passed them. Melanie stared, fascinated. The strange man on the tricycle saw her, and smiled. Melanie thought he looked nice.

'Really,' muttered Councillor Mrs Brace-Girdle disapprovingly.

Mr Majeika could see that the two ladies didn't like the look of him. Obviously he hadn't done the right thing to please *these* Britlanders. Oh dear!

Then a strange thing happened. He noticed that Councillor Mrs Brace-Girdle had a string of sausages in her wheeled shopping-basket, fresh from the butcher's. Mr Majeika looked at those sausages, and the top of his hair began to twitch.

In Walpurgis, the top of his hair had always twitched when he was trying to do a spell. This had always annoyed the other wizards. They said it wasn't dignified.

Surely he wasn't going to do a spell now? The Worshipful Wizard had warned him: *Nothing Walpurgian.*

But yes! The sausages were dancing out of Councillor Mrs Brace-Girdle's basket and all over the pavement.

Councillor Mrs Brace-Girdle and her friend Mrs Sherwood-Greene didn't notice; they were too busy clicking their tongues in disapproval over Mr Majeika's appearance. 'Just ignore him, Melanie,' they said crossly.

Melanie picked up the sausages and waved happily at Mr Majeika. If only he was going to stay in Much Barty, life in that sleepy little village would be *much* more exciting, she thought. But that was too much to hope for.

Hamish Bigmore was getting ready to go to school. Or rather, Hamish Bigmore *wasn't* getting ready to go to school. He was still dawdling over his seven different kinds of breakfast cereal, mixing a little of the Sugared Robots with the Frost Crispies, and then pouring so much milk over the lot that it was quite inedible. He threw it all in the sink, breaking the bowl in the process.

'Come on, Hamish, darling,' cooed his mother, Mrs Pam Bigmore. 'It's the first day at school, and you don't want to be late for your new teacher, do you?'

'New teacher!' muttered Hamish. 'We'll see about that!'

'Now, darling, have you got everything? Lunch-box? Sports bag? Sweeties for break-time? Hanky in case of nose-bleeds? Plasters in case of little grazed knees?'

She bustled out to the car in her high-heeled shoes. Hamish shuffled after her. The car was a white Rolls-Royce with the number-plate BIG 1. Hamish's father had made a lot of money somewhere or other; when asked about it, he would say only that he had 'various business interests'.

'And you will *try*,' said Pam Bigmore, as she started the car, 'you will *try*, won't you, Hamish, to be a better boy this term. Try to be a better little boy for your Mumsy.'

Hamish climbed in and slammed the door, ignoring her.

'I mean, Hamish darling, it was very sad last term. Your poor teacher . . .'

'Going off her rocker?' snarled Hamish. 'Going absolutely and utterly round the twist?'

'Yes,' sighed his mother. 'Poor Miss Jelley.'

'Don't talk rubbish, Mum. It's not *my* fault if they keep wheeling in wally after wally to teach me. I can't wait to see what idiot they've found this term.'

Melanie met Thomas Grey at the school gate. 'I wonder who's going to be our new teacher,' she said.

Thomas sighed. 'I don't much care,' he said. 'The only thing that would really please me was if Hamish Bigmore didn't come back to school.'

The white Rolls-Royce with the number-plate BIG 1. swept up to the gate, nearly knocking down Thomas and Melanie. Hamish's window rolled down electrically and out shot an arm. Thomas's new lunch-box was snatched out of his hands and thrown across the road, where it smashed to bits against the kerb.

'See what I mean?' said Thomas through gritted teeth. 'I'll get him, I will.'

'No you won't,' said Melanie. 'No one ever gets Hamish Bigmore. It's no good complaining about him to Mr Potter – his father's so rich that Mr Potter doesn't dare do a thing. We'll just have to put up with Hamish, like we always do. Look, you can share my lunch-box.'

Mr Potter saw Hamish Bigmore arriving at school, and hid in his study, hoping against hope that a new teacher for Class Three would arrive at the very last minute. Otherwise *he* would have to teach Class Three himself.

The clock struck nine. There was no hope now. Mr Potter swallowed some more Nerve Pills, and went unsteadily up the stairs to Class Three.

17

Outside the school, Mr Majeika had just arrived on his tricycle. He got off, and pushed it through the gate. The lorries, cars and buses were able to get past at last; they roared off, their drivers shouting rude words at him. Mr Majeika waved back cheerily; obviously this was the Britlanders' way of welcoming him.

'*Everything all right, Majeika?*' said the voice of the Worshipful Wizard in his ears.

'Oh yes, sir. This looks a nice quiet place. All very peaceful. I couldn't possibly get into trouble here, could I?'

When Mr Potter came into Class Three, Hamish Bigmore was sitting on top of a desk. Thomas Grey's legs were sticking out from under the lid. Melanie was trying to pull Hamish off the desk. Mr Potter tried to call for quiet, but no one paid any attention, and then the desk fell over and there was a dreadful fight between Thomas and Hamish. Mr Potter tried to separate them, but quickly gave up and retreated to a corner, fingering his bottle of Nerve Pills.

'Your new teacher hasn't arrived yet,' he told Class Three above the din, 'so I'll be teaching you for a few days. Won't that be fun?'

No one paid any attention. And then suddenly Melanie said: 'Look!' and pointed to the window.

Everyone looked, but there was nothing there. 'What did you see?' they asked her.

'There was someone bouncing outside the window.'

'Bouncing outside the window?' said Mr Potter. 'But how could there be? Class Three is upstairs.'

'I know,' said Melanie, 'but there was someone bobbing up and down. And I think I know who it was – that funny man on the trike.'

*

Melanie was right.

Mr Majeika had indeed been bouncing up and down outside the window. No one had told him that, in Britland, you get into a building by walking through the door. In Walpurgis, wizards simply floated into places as they wished, so he was behaving normally. Except that when he had floated up to the window of Class Three, he remembered that he wasn't supposed to do anything Walpurgian. He floated back down to the playground again, looked in his instruction book, and read: 'In Britland, enter all buildings via the door.'

Mr Majeika scratched his head. He couldn't see a door. (The school door was at the side of the building.) He puzzled around the problem. Then it occurred to him that possibly he still had the X-ray vision that all Walpurgians possess. He tried it. Yes, he could see through the walls into the classroom. There was a door in there all right, a cupboard door. Well, if that was the way to do things, he'd do it. He knew he wasn't supposed to do anything Walpurgian, but the situation seemed to require him to magic himself into the cupboard. His hair began to twitch.

Mr Potter was trying to get Class Three to recite the 'Ode to a Nightingale' when there was the most enormous thump in the corner-cupboard. Mr Potter paused, crossed to the cupboard, and opened it.

Inside stood a chap in curious clothes, with hair like a dishmop, and big round glasses. 'How do you do?' said this person. 'I am your new teacher.' He stepped forward, put his arms round Mr Potter, and was about to kiss him on both cheeks when Mr Potter backed away. (Mr Majeika's instruction book said: 'On meeting a Britlander to

19

whom you wish well, clasp them in your arms and kiss both cheeks.')

'New teacher?' Mr Potter blinked uncertainly.

Mr Majeika nodded.

Mr Potter scratched his head. Well, he had hoped for a miracle, and here it was. True, the man did appear to be an escaped lunatic, but beggars couldn't be choosers.

Mr Potter turned to Class Three. 'Well, everyone,' he told them, 'say hello to your new teacher.'

An hour later, at break-time, Mr Potter was standing outside the door of Class Three, talking to Mr Majeika. The fellow looked a bit more normal now, and certainly he'd managed to take Class Three for an hour without being reduced to a ruin by Hamish Bigmore. (Hamish had been so astonished by the way Mr Majeika had arrived that for once he had been behaving himself.)

'Seventy-nine teachers applied for this post,' Mr Potter was telling Mr Majeika. 'All very good teachers, too. And I know nothing about you, Mr –?'

'Majeika,' said Mr Majeika.

'Ah yes,' said Mr Potter. 'Well, Mr Majeika, we'll try you out for a bit, Mr, er, Majeika, and see how you get on. And if all goes well, then the job is yours.'

'Thank you,' said Mr Majeika gratefully. 'I shall do my best.' Something occurred to him. 'But if seventy-nine teachers applied for the job, why didn't one of them get it?'

'Ah well,' said Mr Potter vaguely. 'It was just a small matter of, er, Hamish Bigmore. His father is dreadfully rich, you see, and is always promising to give a great deal of money to the school. So naturally we have to put up with little Hamish. Do please be nice to the little . . .'

20

'Don't worry, Mr Potter,' said Mr Majeika.

Mr Potter passed a weary hand across his brow. 'You see,' he said, 'I wouldn't want you to go the same way as poor Miss Jelley.'

He and Mr Majeika looked gloomily at the classroom door. On it was the name: 'Miss F. Jelley'. Beneath this, Hamish had written: '. . . is frightened of Hamish Bigmore.'

Mr Majeika's hair twitched as he eyed the notice. As Mr Potter watched, the words vanished, and in their place appeared the smartly painted name: 'Mr Majeika'.

'Goodness,' said Mr Potter. 'Very neat. I suppose you do it all with mirrors?' And he went off happily to make himself a cup of herbal tea.

He was still sipping it twenty minutes later when Mr Majeika walked past the open window of his study. 'Dear me!' called Mr Potter. 'Not leaving us already, Mr, er, Majeika?'

'No, Mr Potter. I'm taking Class Three out for a Nature Ramble.'

'Ah,' said Mr Potter. 'Jolly good. Don't, er, bother to hurry back.'

The Nature Ramble had been Melanie's idea. She gathered that the new teacher hadn't seen the Much Barty countryside before, and it seemed a good opportunity to show him around.

Hamish Bigmore was grumbling like blazes as they followed Mr Majeika across the playground.

'Come along, Hamish!' called Mr Majeika.

'But I never *walk* anywhere,' muttered Hamish. 'Never! I'm always driven everywhere, in the Rolls.'

'Well, you're walking today, Hamish,' said Mr Majeika, who was beginning to enjoy being a teacher. It was

21

nice telling children what to do, rather than having elderly wizards always bossing him about.

Hamish saw Mr Majeika's tricycle parked by the school gate. 'What's this silly old thing?' He kicked the tyres.

'That's mine, Hamish,' said Mr Majeika. 'Please leave it alone.'

'Only a silly old granny would ride a thing like that,' grunted Hamish. '*My* bike has got seventeen gears. Still . . .' and he climbed on to the trike, 'it's better than walking!'

He began to pedal off on the trike. Mr Majeika watched him for a moment, and the top of his hair began to twitch. 'Better watch out, Hamish,' he called.

Suddenly the trike veered off at top speed, out of control. The handlebars snatched themselves from Hamish's grip, and the machine careered around the playground like a bucking bronco. It did a figure-of-eight, screeched to a sudden halt, reared its back wheel like a horse, and tossed Hamish on to the ground.

Hamish sat on the tarmac, nursing his sore bottom. 'Owwwww!' he cried.

Mr Potter, watching from his study window, hastily made a dive for the Nerve Pills.

Class Three set off down the village street. Hamish, still rubbing his bruised rear end, shuffled along at the end of the line, giving Mr Majeika some very dirty glances. The old boy had looked a pushover, far easier to reduce to a jelly than even Miss Jelley had been. So what had gone wrong? Why had that stupid old trike behaved so strangely? It was almost like magic.

Councillor Mrs Brace-Girdle strode out of the village hall, with an armful of papers from the Pavements Committee under her arm, and her friend Mrs Sherwood-

Greene in tow. She saw the Class Three procession and came to an immediate halt.

'Good grief! It's that *person* again, Dilys. What on earth is he doing with our children? We must call the police immediately.'

Mrs Sherwood-Greene went to fetch P.C. Bobby, who was on the other side of the village green, trying to teach Trigger to growl. He bustled over, licking his pencil, with his notebook at the ready.

'And where do you think you're going to, children?' called Mrs Brace-Girdle. 'We don't go anywhere with *strangers*, do we, children? Least of all with *tramps* or persons of *that* sort.'

'But he isn't a stranger, Mum,' said Melanie. 'He's our new teacher. We're going to the duck pond to collect tadpoles.'

'A teacher – him?' said Councillor Mrs Brace-Girdle, rocking back on her heels in disbelief. P.C. Bobby, writing in his notebook, tried to remember if 'teacher' was spelt with two e's.

'That's right, madam,' said Mr Majeika respectfully, bowing politely. 'This morning we have Nature Study.'

P.C. Bobby put away his notebook. Councillor Mrs Brace-Girdle glared angrily. 'Well, I shall have to take up the matter with Mr Potter. Someone should certainly have told *me*. I shall raise it with one of my Committees.' She stalked off to make several telephone calls, dragging Mrs Sherwood-Greene with her.

When they got to the duck pond, Mr Majeika told them to line up with their jars, to dip for tadpoles. 'Who's first?' he called.

'Me first,' shouted Hamish Bigmore. 'It's me, 's'me, everyone. I'm first.'

Mr Majeika paid no attention; Thomas Grey was at the head of the queue. 'I haven't got a jar, sir,' he told Mr Majeika. 'They ran out. I've only got this.' He produced a small freezer-bag.

'Don't worry,' said Mr Majeika, and he dipped Thomas's bag in the pond. When he pulled it out it was full of tadpoles.

'Ace!' said Thomas, holding the bag up for everyone to see. 'Some of them have got little arms and legs already. When will they turn into frogs, sir? Next week?'

Mr Majeika scratched his head, not being too knowledgeable about the habits of Britland tadpoles.

Melanie came to his rescue. 'No,' she said, 'it'll take more than a month.'

'Now it's me, 's'me, everyone!' bawled Hamish, who had pushed his way to the front of the queue. ''S'me now, with the biggest jar.' (He had grabbed the biggest one when they were handed out at school.) 'See, everyone! Watch me!'

Hamish elbowed Mr Majeika aside and plunged his jar into the pond. If he had been looking, he would have seen the top of Mr Majeika's hair twitching. *Don't do anything Walpurgian*, the Worshipful Wizard had said, but it was awfully difficult not to do something about a person who behaved as horribly as Hamish.

Mr Majeika's hair twitched again, and suddenly Hamish let out a cry: 'Yeugh!' An unseen force had pulled his arm right into the pond, and when he managed to get it out, it was covered in frog spawn right up to the elbow. 'Yeugh! Frog spawn! I'm *covered* in it.'

Mr Majeika grinned quietly to himself.

'*Majeika!*' came a warning voice in his ear. It was the Worshipful Wizard. Mr Majeika looked around anxiously, but evidently none of the children had heard anything. '*Majeika, what did I tell you? Nothing Walpurgian!*'

24

So, he was being watched from Walpurgis, at least some of the time, when the Worshipful Wizard was awake. That was going to make things extra difficult. Oh dear, oh dear. 'I'm sorry, sir,' he whispered.

Thomas Grey was roaring with laughter to see Hamish trying to wipe the frog spawn off his arm. Suddenly Hamish dug into his pocket for a pencil, and punctured Thomas's freezer-bag, so that water began to spout out. 'Oh no!' cried Thomas. 'My tadpoles'll die.'

Mr Majeika stepped forward and touched the freezer-bag with the end of a finger. When he took it away, the leak had stopped and the bag was as good as new.

Thomas stared at it. 'You can't even see where the hole was,' he said. 'How did you do that, sir?'

For answer, Mr Majeika merely put his finger to his lips.

Melanie came over and stared at the bag.

'Cor, Melanie,' said Thomas, 'it was magical.'

Twenty minutes later, they were back at school. Hamish, conscious that he was not at all on top of the situation today, was in a worse temper than ever. When they passed Mr Majeika's tricycle on the way to the classroom, he gave it a vicious kick.

'Hamish,' warned Mr Majeika, 'leave that alone.'

But Hamish wouldn't. He remembered how the trike had treated him, and decided to get his own back. There was a nice new bell on it which he tried to wrench off.

Mr Majeika was upstairs now, back in Class Three. He leant out of the classroom window. 'Hamish, come upstairs at once, and leave that alone!'

Hamish paid no attention. Reaching in his pocket for the sharp pencil, he dug it into one of the tyres.

Mr Majeika's hair was twitching furiously. He tried to

25

keep control of himself, but the Walpurgian in him was conquering the Britland teacher that he was trying to become. There was no getting away from it, he was a wizard from top to toe. And maybe not so bad a wizard after all. That freezer-bag had mended quite nicely.

Hamish managed to puncture one of the tyres, and set to work on another. 'Hamish, I warned you!' called Mr Majeika. 'Touch that trike once more, and I won't answer for the consequences.'

Hamish paid no attention. Mr Majeika's hair was quite out of control now: the bit at the top wiggled wildly. It was no good; try as he might, a spell was on the way.

Hamish cackled with laughter to see the mess he was making of the trike's tyres. And suddenly there was a flash and a puff of smoke, and when it cleared, Hamish was nowhere to be seen – except for his shoes, which stood by themselves where he had been in the playground.

Mr Majeika passed his hand over his eyes. What had he been thinking of? He was an idiot; he knew he mustn't treat Britland children as if they were Walpurgians. Now what could have happened to the wretched boy? The trouble was, he couldn't remember which spell he had found himself muttering when he finally lost his temper.

'Where's Hamish?' asked Melanie, noticing that things were very quiet in Class Three.

'Oh, he'll be coming back in a moment, I expect,' said Mr Majeika. 'I hope,' he added under his breath.

'Nothing's happened, has it, Majeika?' said a voice in his ear. Evidently the Worshipful Wizard, who must have dozed off, had just woken up again.

Mr Majeika gulped. 'Oh, no, sir, not at all,' he said in a squeaky voice.

'Who are you talking to, sir?' Thomas asked Mr Majeika.

'No one, no one at all, Thomas,' answered Mr Majeika,

wishing he could disappear. Now where on earth was Hamish Bigmore?

'Come over here, sir!' called Melanie, with eyes as big as saucers. 'You won't believe this, Mr Majeika, but one of the tadpoles has already turned into a frog!'

Mr Majeika's mind was on other things. 'Oh yes?' he said vaguely. He wondered what spells he dared try which might bring Hamish Bigmore back.

'Yes, sir, a frog, a really big frog. How on earth did that happen all at once?' asked Melanie.

'It's a very ugly frog,' said Thomas. 'In fact, it's almost as ugly as Hamish Bigmore.'

'Oh yes?' said Mr Majeika again vaguely. Then an awful thought struck him. He stumbled across the classroom and peered into the tank where they had all put the tadpoles. Sure enough, a large ugly frog was crouching on a rock, peering back at him. Its face looked strangely familiar.

'Yes,' said Melanie. 'In fact it looks just like Hamish himself!'

Everyone laughed. Everyone except for Mr Majeika.

There was a knock at the classroom door, and in came Mr Potter. 'Ah, there you are, Majeika. Things still going well?' he asked.

'Oh yes, yes,' answered Mr Majeika with forced jollity. 'Swimmingly well.'

It was the end of afternoon school, and everyone was going home. Mr Majeika was looking very worried indeed. Hamish had not reappeared, and the frog, in its tank, was behaving just the way Hamish always behaved, bounding around, pushing the tadpoles out of the way, and generally looking like a very obstreperous school-boy. Mr Majeika had no doubt at all that it was Hamish. In spare moments, when Class Three were writing in their books, or reading, he tried to rack his brains to remember spells for turning people back into themselves. But of course someone who has failed 'O'-Level Sorcery seventeen times isn't likely to be able to recall the right spell when he wants to. And Mr Majeika didn't know where he could lay his hands on a Spell Book. His own copy was still up there in Walpurgis, and it was no good asking them to send it down, they'd ask what he wanted it for. Oh dear, oh dear, oh dear.

Mr Majeika was definitely in a gloom. In the passage he bumped into Mr Potter. 'Er, Mr Potter,' he said cautiously, 'there's something I have to tell you. One slight problem. Hamish Bigmore . . .' His voice tailed off.

'Ah yes, Hamish Bigmore,' said Mr Potter. 'Well, I did warn you, Majeika. Hamish Bigmore is always a problem. You'll just have to cope as best you can. Always a problem, you know.'

'Yes,' said Mr Majeika sadly, peering at the frog, which he had put into a jam-jar. 'Well, I think he's even more of a problem this time.'

The parents were collecting their children at the school gates, but for once the white Rolls with the number-plate BIG 1 wasn't there; Pam Bigmore was having her hair done, and she had been delayed under the drier. If Hamish had been there to complain, he most certainly *would* have complained, and would probably have persuaded someone else to drive him home (though it was only ten minutes' walk). As it was, there was no trouble.

Councillor Mrs Brace-Girdle was usually too busy with her Committees to collect Melanie, and she wasn't there today, so Melanie went off happily with Thomas. When they saw Mr Majeika climbing on to his trike, clutching the jam-jar with the frog, they ran after him.

28

'Where do you live, Mr Majeika?' they asked him.

'Live?' answered Mr Majeika, blinking distractedly. 'Oh, in the land of Wal ... I mean, well, nowhere in particular. I haven't had time to find anywhere in Much Barty. I was thinking of looking now. Have you got any ideas?'

Melanie thought for a moment. 'Yes,' she said. 'I have.'

She and Thomas led Mr Majeika down the lane behind Thomas's house and up a small hill, at the top of which stood an old windmill. The farmer who owned it was always hoping that some rich city person would come and rent it as a country cottage, but no one ever did, and the signboard that said TO LET had ivy growing all over it.

Mr Majeika looked at the windmill. 'Do you think that will do?' he asked Thomas and Melanie.

'Oh yes,' said Melanie. 'Very nicely.'

'And what do I do now?'

'Well,' said Thomas, 'you're supposed to go to the estate agent, and tell him you want to rent the windmill, and give him some money. Then he'll come here and take down the sign that says TO LET, and put up another that says LET, and then you move in.'

'Hm,' said Mr Majeika, the top of his hair twitching, 'why don't we skip all that and just go on to the last part?'

As he spoke, the signboard swivelled round by itself, so that it now read LET. 'There we are,' said Mr Majeika. 'And now I'll move in.'

'Cor,' said Thomas, 'he *is* magical, Melanie!'

Moving in was even more magical. The furniture arrived through the windows without anyone carrying it. The

29

carpets unrolled themselves, and when Mr Majeika held out his arms, pictures appeared on the walls. In five minutes there was a lovely cosy room with everything anyone could possibly want in a country cottage. Fortunately the Worshipful Wizard must have gone to sleep again, for there were no complaints from Walpurgis.

'Well, here we are, Hamish,' said Mr Majeika brightly to the frog in the jam-jar, putting it down on the table which had just laid itself magically for tea. 'Home, sweet home.'

Thomas and Melanie began to tuck into the tea. There was chocolate cake, chocolate biscuits, all kinds of fizzy drinks, and the most delicious ice-cream.

'You're a wizard, aren't you?' said Thomas, with his mouth full.

'A real live wizard,' said Melanie, beginning her fourth slice of chocolate cake.

'Me?' blinked Mr Majeika. 'Good gracious, no. I'm just an ordinary teacher, really I am.'

'You're a wizard from Walpurgis,' said Thomas.

'Walpurgis? What's that?' spluttered Mr Majeika. 'Never heard of it.'

'It's where all the wizards come from, everyone knows that.'

'Oh, is it?' said Mr Majeika brightly. 'Never heard of it.'

'Nonsense,' said Melanie. 'You can't fool us. We know a wizard when we see one.'

'Well,' said Mr Majeika, 'all right. I admit it. I am.'

The children squealed with delight. 'Cor,' said Thomas. '*Really* magical, Melanie. I told you!'

'But you're not to tell – right?' went on Mr Majeika anxiously. 'Because it's more than my new job is worth to let on.'

'Don't worry,' said Melanie. 'We won't.'

'Promise?'

'We promise,' they said.

'Not a pie-crust promise, I hope?' said Mr Majeika.

'Pie-crust?' asked Thomas.

'Quickly made, easily broken,' said Mr Majeika.

The children shook their heads. 'Come on,' said Melanie, 'let's do it properly.'

All three of them joined hands around the tea-table. '"Here's a promise strong and deep,"' they all chanted,

> 'And a promise meant to keep.
> And if any time we stray,
> May our tongues be snatched away.'

'There,' added Melanie, 'now your secret's safe with us.'

'But there's one more thing we need to know,' said Thomas. 'Why did you call the frog Hamish when you spoke to it just now?'

'Well,' said Mr Majeika, 'can't you guess?'

The children shook their heads.

'I can't tell you out loud,' said Mr Majeika, 'because –' and his voice sank to a whisper, '– *they* may be listening up in Walpurgis. But I'll tell you as quietly as I can.'

He whispered in Melanie's ear. 'Hamish is *what*?' Melanie said, incredulously. She leant over and whispered to Thomas.

'I don't believe it!' shouted Thomas, bursting out laughing. 'Hamish is a *frog*!'

He and Melanie fell about laughing helplessly.

'Ssh!' said Mr Majeika. 'And it's not funny.'

'Yes it is,' they said. 'It's the funniest thing we've ever heard.'

'Well,' said Mr Majeika, 'it is rather what he deserved. But it makes it all very difficult for me.'

'But you're a wizard,' said Thomas. 'Change him back.'

'I would if I knew the right spell. But I *never* know the

right spell. That's why they kicked me out of Walpurgis and made me a teacher instead.'

'With a frog for a pupil,' said Thomas, laughing till the tears ran down his cheeks.

'It isn't funny, Thomas!' said Mr Majeika.

'Wait till his Mummy finds out,' laughed Melanie. 'Finds out that her little darling Hamish is a –'

But just at that moment, Thomas, who had been flailing about wildly on the sofa, still helpless with laughter, shot out an arm and knocked over the jar in which the frog was sitting. With a bound, the frog leapt across the room and was out through the door.

'Oh no!' cried Mr Majeika. 'Hamish! Come back!'

'Hamish! Hamish!' called the children, rushing out on to the steps of the windmill. But Hamish was nowhere to be seen.

'Cor,' said Thomas. 'That's torn it.'

Pam Bigmore was holding a little drinks party on the patio round her swimming-pool. Hamish usually spoilt her parties by being rude to her friends, but today there was no sign of him, and though Pam had worried a little when she eventually drove up to the school gate in the white Rolls and found no one there, she had to admit that it was peaceful without her little darling.

'Dilys,' she called to her friend, Mrs Sherwood-Greene, 'do mix some more egg-nog.'

'No more for me, thank you, Pamela,' muttered Councillor Mrs Brace-Girdle, who was reclining on a li-lo in Mrs Bigmore's swimming-pool. The first glass of egg-nog, Mrs Brace-Girdle thought to herself, had tasted like something the cat had sicked up. She had poured it surreptitiously into the water, and now it was slowly clouding the swimming-pool with an oily trail.

Pam Bigmore patted her new hair-do, and thought what a snob Bunty Brace-Girdle was. Just because her husband travelled to London each day and worked in the City! Neither of the Brace-Girdles would even talk to Ronnie Bigmore, Hamish's father. She'd even overheard Mr Brace-Girdle saying he thought Ronnie had been mixed up in that gold bullion robbery at Heathrow. Really! Just because Ronnie had one or two friends who weren't always on the best of terms with the police . . . Still, it was quite a *coup* to have Bunty Brace-Girdle floating about in her swimming-pool. Bunty (though few people dared call her by her first name) did have a lot of influence in the village, with all her Committees, there was no denying that.

'Some children to see you, madam,' said Mrs Vim, who came in to 'do' for the Bigmores twice a week.

Melanie Brace-Girdle and Thomas Grey came out on to the patio.

Pam Bigmore eyed them without enthusiasm. Scruffy kids, even if one of them was Bunty Brace-Girdle's daughter. All these snobby parents always dressed their children in worn-out hand-me-downs, whereas Hamish had *nothing* that wasn't new.

'What do you want?' she said to the children suspiciously. 'Hamish isn't here.'

'Er – we know, Mrs Bigmore,' said Melanie. She and Thomas had decided to come and reassure Hamish's mother, in case she decided to call the police. They had left Mr Majeika looking frantically for the frog; it wouldn't do any good if P.C. Bobby got involved as well.

'We know he isn't here, Mrs Bigmore,' said Thomas. 'We came to tell you that he's – he's playing with friends.'

Pam Bigmore whipped off her diamanté sunglasses suspiciously. 'That can't be the truth!' she snapped. 'My Hamish hasn't got any friends!'

'He has now,' said Melanie. 'Lots.'

Pam eyed them carefully. 'And what are these friends called?' She didn't want Hamish mixing with any of the other rabble in Class Three. A rough lot they were, they might hurt him.

'Er, tadpoles,' said Thomas quietly to himself.

Melanie kicked him.

Suddenly something hopped across the patio. Thomas saw it out of the corner of his eye. 'It's *him*, Melanie!' he whispered. 'Look!'

When Melanie looked, the frog had gone. But there was a trail of webbed footprints leading across the patio towards the pool.

'Everything all right, Majeika?' asked the voice of the Worshipful Wizard in Mr Majeika's ear.

'Oh, yes, sir, wonderful, wonderful! A good first day at school, all terribly nice.' Mr Majeika paused to get his breath back. For the last half-hour he had been struggling through the undergrowth in the wood behind the windmill, clutching a saucer of milk in one hand, and calling out, 'Hamish! Hamish! Good boy, Hamish! Come to teacher for your tea!' Once or twice he thought he had spotted the frog; it seemed to be making towards some houses on the other side of the wood. But he could never catch up with it.

He stopped and mopped his brow.

'Just out for a walk, Majeika? Taking the evening air, eh?'

'Oh, y-yes, sir. That's right, sir. Good-night, sir.'

'Good-night, Majeika.'

Mr Majeika sighed. It was getting late. An idea occurred to him. He had spotted his Spell Book among the furniture in the windmill; they must have sent it down from Walpurgis by mistake – the Worshipful Wizard wouldn't have wanted him to have it; but it had certainly turned up. And there was just a chance that he might find, somewhere in its pages, the right spell for the present situation.

He struggled back through the undergrowth, reached the windmill, found the Spell Book, and collapsed into a chair. For a few moments he turned the pages in silence, and then he suddenly brightened up.

'Ah!' he said aloud. For there it was, plain on the page: 'For turning Frogs into Boys'. He read it carefully, then sighed. What it said was this:

> Boys can be turned into frogs only on dry land. To reverse this spell, simply put frog into lake, river or swimming-pool.

'But I don't know where the blooming frog is!' said Mr Majeika.

Councillor Mrs Brace-Girdle was just wondering whether it would be rude to get out of the pool and go home – the water was terribly cold, and Mrs Bigmore's drinks quite undrinkable – when something clammy landed on top of her, and she screamed. 'Aarggh! There's a frog! A frog in the pool!'

So indeed there had been, but when the frog jumped off her and into the water, there was a huge ripple and, where the frog had been, there was Hamish.

'Ha, ha!' shouted Hamish. ''S'me, everyone! Look at me! 'S'me, Mummy, 's'me!'

'Hamish, darling,' crooned Pam Bigmore, helping her son out of the swimming-pool, and wondering how he came to be there fully clothed, and why he was there at all. She finally decided that she must have drunk too much egg-nog; it had clouded her brain.

Towels were fetched, and dry clothes, and in a few moments Hamish had been put to bed with hot-water bottles and a thermometer. He did not seem to know what he was doing in the swimming-pool, or where he had been before that, though he muttered darkly about Mr Majeika.

'Well, *that's* all right, then,' whispered Melanie to Thomas, as her mother drove them home from the Bigmores'. 'You'd better slip out when you get home, and tell Mr Majeika. He'll be awfully relieved.'

'Yes,' whispered Thomas. 'But really, Hamish wasn't at all a bad frog. Wouldn't it have been nice if . . .' He sighed, and thought gloomily about having to put up with Hamish for the rest of term. Still, with a wizard for a teacher, there might be other ways of keeping Hamish under control . . .

2

AND MAY THE BEST BARTYAN WIN

No one had thought to provide Mr Majeika with an alarm clock – in Walpurgis they had not heard of such ingenious gadgets – so the Worshipful Wizard, anxious that Failed Apprentice Wizard Majeika should not be late for his job at St Barty's School in the little Britland village of Much Barty, made sure that he had a personal alarm call.

'*Out of bed, Majeika!*' his voice thundered in poor Mr Majeika's ear.

Mr Majeika, who had lashed up a hammock for a bed in his new windmill home, tumbled out of it on to the floor. 'Thank you, sir,' he said humbly, as he picked himself up. He had hoped, when he got down to Britland, that he would be allowed to get on with things as best he could. But clearly he was never going to be left in peace.

'*Breakfast!*' ordered the Worshipful Wizard. '*Come along, now! We don't want you late for school.*'

'No, sir,' muttered Mr Majeika, pulling on his clothes.

He stumbled out of the windmill and plucked an armful of nettles, thistles and other spiky-looking wild plants – the sort of thing every self-respecting Walpurgian breakfasts off daily. He hurried back in, crammed them into his Walpurgian Juice Extractor, switched on, held a bowl to

37

catch the green gooey stuff that came out the other end, and was about to swallow it when the Worshipful Wizard interrupted his thoughts again.

'Majeika! We don't feel you should eat a Walpurgian breakfast. Remember, you're a Britlander now!'

There was a thump, and several articles landed out of nowhere on to Mr Majeika's breakfast table. There was a box labelled Corn Flakes, a bag marked Castor Sugar, and a packet of Long Life Milk.

'That's what Britlanders eat,' said the voice of the Worshipful Wizard. *'Come on, Majeika, get on with it!'*

Mr Majeika examined the corn flakes, the milk and the sugar, all of which looked very strange to him. He tore open the top of the corn flakes packet, peered inside and, after a moment's consideration, poured all the sugar and milk into it.

He tried tasting the result, eating with his hands.

It wasn't very nice.

'I'll finish it on the way to school,' he muttered in case the Worshipful Wizard was still listening; and hurrying out of the windmill he put the corn flakes packet (from which milk was now dripping) in the box at the back of his tricycle.

Hamish Bigmore was having breakfast. He had emptied four packets of corn flakes all over the breakfast table in the hope of finding the little plastic submarines that were supposed to be in them. He could only find one of them, so he was in a very bad temper.

'And how are you getting on with that new teacher of yours, Hamish darling?' asked his mother, Pam Bigmore, filing her nails over her bowl of muesli, and peering at Hamish across the mountain of spilt corn flakes. 'Being a good boy for him, are you?'

Hamish glared at her. He still had no idea how he had come to be in the swimming-pool fully clothed, but he was sure Mr Majeika was behind it, and he wasn't going to let the new teacher get away with any further nonsense, even if the silly fellow did have a trick or two up his sleeve. It would take more than a party conjuror to get the upper hand over Hamish Bigmore.

When Mr Majeika reached St Barty's School, Mr Potter the headmaster was on a ladder at the gate, hanging up a big sign which said:

NEXT SATURDAY: SCHOOL FÊTE

Mr Majeika looked at the notice, trying out the strange word to himself. How might it be pronounced? Feet? Fetty? Fett?

Milk was trickling out of the back of his tricycle, so he rescued the box of corn flakes, and looked for a dust-bin – hoping that the Worshipful Wizard wasn't watching.

'Ah, there you are, Majeika,' said Mr Potter, climbing down the ladder, and eyeing the damp box of corn flakes. 'I see you've started collecting for next Saturday already. That's the thing, all contributions for stalls very welcome. I'll have a word with you about it later.' He strode off to his study feeling quite cheerful. Really, he could keep off the Nerve Pills now this chap Majeika was around; things seemed to be going quite smoothly. Even Hamish Bigmore had been quiet yesterday; for much of the time you'd have thought he wasn't even there.

'Fetty? Fett?' muttered Mr Majeika to himself, still staring at the sign and clutching the corn flakes.

'It's not a Fetty, it's a Fate,' said Melanie, who had just arrived at the school.

39

'It's a French word,' added Thomas, who was just behind her, 'and it means a Festive Day.'

'Do you have festive days in Walpurgis, Mr Majeika?' asked Melanie.

Mr Majeika's face lit up. 'Do we? I'll say we do! We have one each Walpurgis Night, when we light bonfires everywhere, and make great cauldrons of Rat and Nettle Soup, and put on war paint, and dance wildly round and round – and that's just the beginning! It gets much noisier later. Is that what a Fetty – I mean a Fate – is like? Oh, I can't wait till Saturday!'

Melanie shook her head. 'Yours sounds much more fun. I'm afraid ours is just grown-ups pretending to be all sweet and charming, instead of being bossy like they usually are.'

'And we have Stalls,' added Thomas, 'where you buy things that aren't the slightest use.'

'And cakes that no one could possibly eat.'

'And everyone's old books that no one would ever want to read.'

'And play silly games that everyone pretends to enjoy.'

'And that's a Fate?' asked Mr Majeika. 'Oh dear, I think I'd rather be in Walpurgis.'

Mr Potter came out of his study and crossed the playground, carrying a huge silver cup on a pedestal.

'And what's that?' asked Mr Majeika. 'Is that part of the Fate?' Melanie nodded. 'Do you drink Rat and Nettle Soup out of it?'

Thomas shook his head. 'That's the cup for the Best Bartyan. It's awarded every year at the Fête.'

'Oh,' said Mr Majeika. 'We don't have that in Walpurgis. It doesn't sound very exciting.'

'It's very silly,' said Melanie. 'It's awarded to whoever is judged the most helpful person in the village. And you can guess who always wins it.'

'Her mother,' said Thomas scornfully. 'It's all her Committees. People think she's being terribly helpful – though, if you ask me, she's wasting everyone's time, is Councillor Mrs Brace-Girdle.'

Melanie nodded gloomily. 'She wins it year after year. She'd be terribly offended if she wasn't chosen as Best Bartyan.'

'Best Bartyan,' said Mr Majeika thoughtfully. 'And I was always the worst wizard. I wonder . . . Do you think that if – if *I* won the cup this year, they would be pleased with me up in Walpurgis? You see, if I behave frightfully well down here as a teacher, I think they'll let me go back to Walpurgis, and I can continue with my studies as a wizard after all. And it just occurred to me that this cup – if I could win it – well, it might be just the thing to prove to them how very good I was!'

Thomas and Melanie looked at each other, and then at Mr Majeika, in his odd clothes, with his odd appearance, and with milk trickling down his trousers from the corn flakes packet which he was still clutching.

'You, sir!' laughed Thomas. '*You'll* never be Best Bartyan!'

'Not a chance,' said Melanie.

'But I must try,' said Mr Majeika earnestly. 'Do help me to try.'

'Well,' said Melanie, 'if you must, then I suppose there's no stopping you. Perhaps you could magic yourself into winning it?'

Mr Majeika shook his head. 'Oh no, that wouldn't be playing the game. And they'd discover all about it in Walpurgis. No, I've got to try and win it by Britland rules. So what should I do first?'

'Well,' said Melanie, 'I know they're having a Fête Committee meeting after school this afternoon, at Mrs Bigmore's house. Why don't you go along and ask them if you can help? They always want more grown-ups to do the stalls and things like that. It would be a start.'

*

41

The Fête Committee was already in session when Mr Majeika arrived at the Bigmore house on his tricycle. The house was surrounded by high walls, and the gates were shut and locked; Ronnie Bigmore, Hamish's father, liked to protect himself against certain 'business associates'.

Mr Majeika found a box labelled 'Entryphone: Press and Speak', with a little hand-written card on it that said: 'Bigmore Residence'. He pressed the button and spoke.

'Open, Sesame,' he said. But the gates, which were not Walpurgian, did not budge.

Instead, from the little box, came a tinny voice: 'Who is it?' Pam Bigmore was at the other end of the Entryphone.

Mr Majeika almost jumped out of his skin. The gates seemed to be speaking to him!

'Hello!' called Pam Bigmore's voice.

Mr Majeika looked all around him, but he could not see the speaker anywhere. Inside the house, Pam Bigmore, tired of shouting 'Hello', pressed the button which opened the gates by remote control. (She had decided that it must be the Vicar, who never knew how to work the Entryphone properly.)

Mr Majeika stared in amazement as the gates swung apart. This was Britland magic indeed! He set off up the drive.

While he was on his way, Councillor Mrs Brace-Girdle, chairing the Fête Committee which was gathered on the Bigmores' patio, raised the question of flags. Did anyone remember what had happened to the flags after last year's Fête? Pam Bigmore said she thought they were in her garage; she would go and have a look. But then the phone rang, and she went to take the call; in the meanwhile Councillor Mrs Brace-Girdle, who was always thoroughly

42

nosey about other people's property, decided *she* would go and have a look in the Bigmores' garage herself.

The garage door was opened by a photo-electric beam, so that when the white Rolls with the number-plate BIG 1 came up the drive the door would open and shut by itself. At that moment the garage was standing open, and Councillor Mrs Brace-Girdle went inside and started to root around. A few seconds later, Mr Majeika, walking up the drive, passed the photo-electric beam, causing the door to shut.

He saw it shut and, again, he stared in disbelief. This Britland magic was everywhere! How did they do it?

He went up to the front door and rang the bell – not realizing that he had just shut Councillor Mrs Brace-Girdle in the garage.

Pam Bigmore came back on to the patio to find that Mr Majeika had added himself to the Committee which, beside herself, consisted of Mr Potter, Mrs Sherwood-Greene, and a lady in a hat decorated with fruit.

'Ah, hello, Mr –'

'Majeika,' said Mr Majeika.

'Ah, yes, Majeika,' said Mr Potter, recognizing his new teacher.

'Pleased to meet you, Mr Majeika,' said Pam Bigmore. 'Do help yourself to nibbles.' She pointed at the dish of twiglets and other savoury bits on the table. 'Now, I wonder where Mrs Brace-Girdle has got to? We can't do much without her.'

There was a distant banging and shouting from the garage, but no one connected it with the absence of Mrs Brace-Girdle. Mr Majeika, remembering the offer of 'nibbles', began picking at the nearest thing that looked edible: the fruit on his neighbour's hat.

43

'I expect dear Bunty is answering a call of nature,' said Mr Potter benignly. 'We can get on without her. Now, the next item on the agenda is Stalls and Entertainments. As for Entertainments, we have, of course, the Much Barty Silver Band (somebody must really find them some polish for their instruments this year), and I've put myself down for a spot of handbell ringing, since it always seems popular every year.'

Everyone who remembered Mr Potter playing 'Edelweiss' on his handbells at previous school fêtes winced at the thought.

'As for Stalls, Miss Haddock has agreed to man Savoury Flans, and oh, mentioning entertainments, we mustn't forget the Queen of the Fête Float. I think Councillor Mrs Brace-Girdle had someone in mind for this year's Queen?'

'Yes,' said Pam Bigmore firmly. 'Me.'

Mrs Sherwood-Greene looked very doubtful at this, but down went Mrs Bigmore on Mr Potter's list as Queen of the Fête.

(Out in the garage, Mrs Brace-Girdle had broken the heel of her shoe in banging it against the door, and her voice was quite hoarse from screaming: 'Let me out!')

The Committee meeting was proceeding much more quickly than usual: it occurred to Mr Potter how much time Mrs Brace-Girdle usually wasted with her Agendas and Any Other Business and all the rest of it. 'Not much more to sort out,' he said. 'Though we don't appear to have a volunteer for the raffle table.'

There was a moment's silence, and then Mr Majeika saw his chance. His hand shot up. 'I'll do it, Mr Potter!' A vision of the Best Bartyan Cup rose before his eyes. He'd show them all! He'd run the whole Fetty single-handed.

'Thank you, Majeika,' said Mr Potter. 'Now, Toffee Apples Stall, anyone?'

'I'll do it!' cried Mr Majeika.

'As well as the Raffle?' asked Mr Potter doubtfully. 'Well, I suppose if we set them up next to each other . . . Then there's Candy Floss?'

'Me!' cried Mr Majeika.

'Well . . . if you think it's possible, Majeika. Popcorn? Anyone fancy that?'

'Me, me! I'll do it all, Mr Potter!'

'Well, well,' said Mr Potter, 'you seem determined to be helpful, Majeika. And far be it from me to stop you, if you can really manage it all. But of course there's one thing you needn't do. Dear Bunty Brace-Girdle – can't think where she's got to – always runs the Cake Stall herself.'

'Oh, Mr Potter, can't *I* make a cake for it?' panted Mr Majeika. 'I do like to be helpful!'

'What's he want to make a cake for?' said Melanie. 'Hasn't he got enough to do with all those other stalls?'

'He's simply determined to do everything,' said Thomas. 'The way he's going on, he really might win the Best Bartyan Cup after all. Your mum would be furious if he did.'

'She's furious enough with him anyway,' said Melanie. 'She thinks he shut her in Mrs Bigmore's garage, though I can't think how. She was in there for three hours. Now, does he really want rotten pears?'

'That's what he said,' answered Thomas. They were gathering ingredients for a cake in the woodland behind Mr Majeika's windmill. A Walpurgian cake.

'Can't think what people are going to make of *this*,' said Melanie, as she and Thomas brought their pickings back to the windmill. 'He can't seriously expect to become Best Bartyan if he makes people eat such stuff. Still . . .'

45

They went into the kitchen – where Mr Majeika was already mixing ingredients – and helped him stir it all up. 'Two sacks of sawdust,' Thomas read out from the recipe book. 'Pint of ditchwater. Four ounces of – oh, I say, not really!'

'Let me see,' said Mr Majeika, and Thomas passed over the recipe. 'Yes, that's right, four ounces of worms. I've got them here.'

'Two pounds of pips,' said Melanie, 'and here's the bag of nettles and berries, and have you got the bats' toe-nails?'

Mr Majeika nodded. 'And finally,' he said, 'that special ingredient which gives it the real Walpurgian taste. A squeeze of slug juice.'

'Yuck!' said Thomas. 'Are you really going to cook it all?'

'Cook?' said Mr Majeika disgustedly. 'Certainly not! In Walpurgis we like our cake – raw!'

He stirred it all together and scooped out a handful. 'Mm, delicious,' he declared. 'Now it's time for you both to try some. What, you're not going already, are you?'

'We'll stay if you don't mind us not eating it,' said Melanie. 'I just don't think you've quite adjusted to the ways of Much Barty, sir. If you really want to win that Best Bartyan Cup, you're going to have to change your ways a lot by Saturday, Mr Majeika.'

The sun shone brightly on the day of the Fête, and the very, very old Earl Barty, the local Lord of the Manor, who had come to perform the official opening, smiled cheerfully at everyone as Councillor Mrs Brace-Girdle pushed him around in his wheelchair. Mrs Brace-Girdle made a short speech welcoming him but, by the time she had finished, the Earl had dozed off.

Mrs Brace-Girdle tapped him on the shoulder. 'What? Eh?' said the old Earl, waking up with a start. 'Bunty! How nice to see you, my dear. What on earth are you doing here?' (Mrs Brace-Girdle had played on the Earl's knee when she was just a tiny young thing.)

She whispered in his ear: 'You're supposed to open the Fête!'

'What? Ah, yes,' said the Earl. 'Well, carry on, you chaps.' And he fell fast asleep again.

Councillor Mrs Brace-Girdle tapped him on the shoulder. 'Come along, now,' she said briskly. 'You've got to go round all the stalls, and chat to everyone, you know. But maybe you'd like something to wake you up first? I'll take you over to the refreshment tent and get you a large –'

'Oh, rather,' said the Earl, waking up properly for the first time. 'And not too much soda in it.'

'– cup of tea,' concluded Mrs Brace-Girdle.

'Oh,' said the Earl disappointedly, as she wheeled him off. 'Well, if that's all there is . . .'

'Now, everyone,' called Mr Potter through the microphone, 'to make things start with a swing, here's Class Three to thrill us with some Country Dancing.'

He put on a very scratchy old record of 'Skip To My Lou', as the whole of Class Three – except Hamish Bigmore – shuffled in front of the loudspeakers and began to do a dance that Mrs Brace-Girdle had taught them.

'This is awful,' muttered Thomas to Melanie.

Up on the stage, in front of his microphone, Mr Potter privately was inclined to agree. He looked hopefully at his watch. 'In two hours,' he muttered to himself, 'it'll be all over.'

There was a disturbance at the front of the crowd. Kicking and screaming, Hamish Bigmore was being dragged into the dance by his mother. 'Don't talk nonsense, Hamish,' Pam Bigmore was saying. 'Dancing *isn't* pansy.'

47

'Don't they look smart, ladies and gentlemen?' cooed Mr Potter into the microphone. 'And now, here to trip the light fantastic with his partner, pretty little Fiona Nobbs-Johnson, comes the ever-popular young Hamish Bigmore.'

Pam Bigmore smirked at Mr Potter, and made up her mind to persuade her husband Ronnie that it was time to give the school that half a million pounds he was always promising. 'Ever-popular.' That was the sort of thing she loved to hear about her little Hamish.'

But the ever-popular Hamish Bigmore was not so popular with pretty little Fiona Nobbs-Johnson. He had just trodden, very heavily and quite deliberately, on her toes, and when she tried to run off to her mother for comfort, Hamish caught hold of her dress so that it ripped right down the back.

Mrs Nobbs-Johnson removed tearful Fiona, casting angry glances at Pam Bigmore, who of course maintained that the whole thing was somehow Fiona's fault. The country dance broke up in disarray.

'I'm sure we all wish that such a pretty dance could have gone on for ever, don't we?' cooed Mr Potter into his microphone. 'Now, enjoy yourselves, everyone. And don't forget that the watchword this afternoon is spend, spend, spend!' Privately, he looked again at his watch. One hour and fifty-five minutes. At this rate, he might still last it out without having to resort to the Nerve Pills.

'He's running the toffee apple stall, the popcorn, the candy floss, and the raffle, and probably several other stalls he's forgotten about. I can't think how he'll do it – but if he does manage it, he really might get that Best Bartyan Cup.' Melanie was standing by the candy floss stall. She and Thomas were waiting for Mr Majeika.

He rushed up. 'Hope I'm not too late,' he panted. 'I was just helping Mr Potter to wind up the gramophone. Ah, here comes my first customer.'

It was Hamish Bigmore, being consoled by his mother for 'that horrid little girl' being so nasty to him in the country dancing. 'Here, Hamish, pet, let's buy you a toffee apple.'

'No!' growled Hamish. 'I don't want to waste time with *his* rotten stuff. Knowing him, it's probably poisoned. I want to *win* something. I've got to win everything at this Fête!'

He dragged his mother off, pausing only to grab a balloon that Thomas had just bought. Thomas was going to chase him and get it back, but Melanie restrained him. 'No, Thomas, don't start a fight now. We want everything to go as well as possible, to give Mr Majeika a chance to win that cup. Look, we ought to buy some toffee apples from him, so that he can make lots of money for the Fête.'

'How much are they?' Thomas asked Mr Majeika.

'Ten pence each,' said Mr Majeika.

'A bit small, aren't they?' said Thomas, examining them.

Mr Majeika looked at them. 'Let's see what I can do,' he said, and Thomas and Melanie noticed that his hair was twitching.

'Oh, do be careful,' said Melanie. 'Don't do anything dangerous, please, Mr Majeika.'

But Mr Majeika had already picked up the tray of toffee apples and turned his back for a moment. When he turned round again, the toffee apples had grown to the size of footballs.

'There you are,' said Mr Majeika proudly. 'That's a good ten pence worth.'

And in five minutes the toffee apple stall had sold out.

*

Hamish Bigmore was managing to win everything, by the very simple method of pushing everyone else aside and cheating like mad. He queue-jumped at the Lucky Dip; he nearly suffocated himself in the bran tub, but finally came up with the biggest parcel he could find in it. At the shooting gallery he climbed over the barrier and stood six inches from the target, driving the protesting proprietor away by threatening him with the gun, and then helping himself to the prizes. At Pin The Tail On The Donkey, he put the blindfold on Mrs Sherwood-Greene, who was in charge, and pinned half a dozen tails in the right place, claiming a prize for each of them. Soon Pam Bigmore was loaded down with goldfish in plastic bags, gigantic orange teddy bears, and outsize balloons. ''S'me, 's'me!' Hamish called to everyone. 'Look how much I've won!'

'Isn't he clever?' cooed Pam Bigmore. 'Isn't he a clever little boy?'

Protesting stall owners complained to Mr Potter, and demanded that Hamish Bigmore and his mother be ejected from the Fête, but Mr Potter shooed them all away. 'Now, now, we can't offend dear Mrs Bigmore, who is to be our Queen of the Fête in the highlight of the afternoon – the Much Barty Ladies' Float.' Meanwhile Mr Potter went on surreptitiously looking at his watch. One hour and thirty minutes. Perhaps he *would* need a handful of those Nerve Pills after all.

Mr Majeika was just about managing to run all his stalls at once – literally to 'run' them, because he had to scamper wildly between them all to serve his customers. And even that wasn't enough for him. When Mr Potter announced that the Much Barty ladies were about to give a demonstration of Maypole Dancing, he rushed over to join in the fun, leaving Thomas and Melanie to mind the popcorn, the candy floss, and the raffle.

Melanie and Thomas couldn't really see what was happening through the crowd, but evidently Mr Majeika was throwing himself into the Maypole Dancing as if it were a Festive Day in Walpurgis. Melanie could hear some titters of laughter at first when he joined the dancing ladies, and some angry shouts from her mother, Councillor Mrs Brace-Girdle, who of course had organized the Maypole and hadn't planned for any men to join in, let alone the outrageous 'tramp' whom Mr Potter had foolishly taken on as Class Three's teacher. From the cheers and applause of the crowd, however, it was clear that Mr Majeika was soon the star of the show. It appeared that he had got in an awful muddle with his maypole ribbon, because Melanie and Thomas could see the top of the pole teetering to and fro; and at the very end, the crowd parted and they caught a brief glimpse of Mr Majeika waving the pole himself – he seemed to be carrying it around as part of the dance. When the music ended there was a terrific cheer.

'What an exhibition!' Mrs Brace-Girdle fumed to Mr Potter.

'Yes, indeed,' said Mr Potter proudly. 'I interviewed seventy-nine teachers before I managed to find him.'

'Errhrrrm!' Mr Potter cleared his throat into the microphone, deafening several old ladies. 'And now, as our festivities begin to draw towards their climax –' he looked at his watch, yes, only an hour left! '– it's time for an event you've all been waiting for. Yes, it's time to draw the raffle tickets! I hope you've all seen the display on Mr Majeika's raffle table, eh? Well, if you haven't yet inspected the prizes, hurry over and take a look, because we're about to make the draw.'

Mr Majeika had just got his breath back from the Maypole Dancing and was stoking up the candy floss machine with more pink sugar when he heard Mr Potter's announcement. 'Whoops! I'd better run over to the raffle,' he muttered, 'in case anyone wants to buy more tickets. Could you two please look after the candy floss? It's quite easy to work – just put a stick into the bowl, and the floss stuff gathers on it.' Off he rushed.

Thomas and Melanie looked at each other, shrugged their shoulders, and began to make candy floss.

'And what a galaxy of raffle prizes we have for you!' announced Mr Potter into the microphone. 'There's a bottle of Mrs Skidmore's parsnip wine, once again – and Mrs Skidmore assures us that this year it won't blow up when you take it home! And we have, er, a bar of chocolate, some nice flowers and, for the first prize, two front-row seats for Mrs Hebblethwaite's next production of *Brigadoon* by the Much Barty Operatic Society, in the village hall. So those are the prizes, and now I'm going to ask Councillor Mrs Brace-Girdle, as Chairman of the Fête Committee, to draw the winning tickets.'

Mrs Brace-Girdle plunged her arm into the bag of tickets.

''S'me, everyone!' called out Hamish Bigmore. ''S'me! I've won!'

'You can't have won yet, Hamish,' said Thomas, who was standing near him. 'They haven't even called out the numbers of the winning tickets.'

Hamish stuck out his tongue at Thomas. 'Whatever the number is, silly, I *must* have won! Look how many tickets my mum bought me!' And he held up a fistful of about a hundred tickets.

It was just at that moment that the candy floss ran out. Melanie signalled over to Mr Majeika. 'We've run out!' she mouthed.

Mr Majeika nodded, and Melanie saw the top of his hair twitching. 'He's going to magic some more,' she whispered to Thomas.

'Oh no!' said Thomas. 'Stand back! There's bound to be trouble.'

'And the winning number,' announced Mr Potter, 'is –'

' 'S'me, 's'me!' called Hamish. 'It *must* be me!'

'– one hundred and thirty-three.'

Hamish looked down at his tickets. Number one hundred and thirty-three wasn't there.

'Here!' called a voice. It was Thomas, holding up the winning ticket – the only one he had bought.

Everybody clapped – and Hamish Bigmore leapt upon Thomas and snatched the ticket. ' 'S'me! 'S'me! I *told* you it would be me!'

'Why, you little –' shouted Thomas, and made a dive for Hamish.

But just at that moment there was a small explosion behind him.

Mr Majeika had indeed magicked more candy floss – far too much of it. The bowl of the machine was filling up with more and more pink goo, and now it had burst out: an enormous pink avalanche which rose into the air and flopped down again, right on top of Hamish Bigmore. Thomas, sensing trouble, had ducked out of the way just in time, but Hamish got the full force of it. ' 'S'me! 'S'me! I've got the winning ticket!' continued his voice, but nothing could be seen of him except a pink mountain from which a hand stuck out, holding the ticket.

Carefully, Thomas removed the ticket and took it to Mr Potter to claim his prize.

'And now,' announced Mr Potter, 'we come to another star event. Our very own Police Constable Bobby will

53

give a demonstration, together with his splendid police dog Trigger, of How To Catch A Burglar.'

There was a ripple of applause, and P.C. Bobby stepped to the front of the crowd, leading Trigger, who looked half asleep.

'He's eaten a whole can of Woofit for his lunch,' P.C. Bobby confided to Melanie, 'so I don't reckon he'll do much harm to no burglar. Never mind, good old Trigger.' And he patted the rather daft-looking dog affectionately.

'Now,' continued Mr Potter, 'we need a volunteer to play the part of the burglar – someone who doesn't mind being chased round the field, and then being brought down in a tackle by P.C. Bobby and Trigger.'

'Me, Mr Potter, I'll do it, please let me do it!' It was, of course, Mr Majeika, bustling once more to the front of the crowd.

'Couldn't we find someone else?' muttered Councillor Mrs Brace-Girdle, who had had quite enough of Mr Majeika for one afternoon.

But Mr Majeika had already got hold of the sack of dog-biscuits that P.C. Bobby hoped would lure the overfed Trigger into chasing the 'burglar'.

'On your marks, Mr Majeika!' called Mr Potter. 'Get ready, go! Oh, I say! Watch him go now! Yes, there he goes. Full speed ahead!'

Mr Potter was referring to Mr Majeika, who was indeed running at full speed round the field, carrying the sack. Not so Trigger, who had lain down happily and gone to sleep. Eventually Mr Majeika panted back to Trigger and the Police Constable.

'By jove,' announced Mr Potter, 'I'm sure we all feel a lot safer knowing Trigger's here to protect our valuables.'

'This won't do,' Mr Majeika whispered to Melanie. 'I'll have to wake that dog up somehow.' And his hair began to twitch.

In an instant, Trigger leapt out of his sleep and was snarling ferociously, like some underfed Alsatian who has just spotted a nice juicy tabby cat. Mr Majeika sprinted off at the double but Trigger was right behind him, snarling and snapping at his heels.

Melanie was biting her nails. 'This is serious,' she said. 'He'll get hurt. Why doesn't he do some magic to stop it?'

The crowd, thoroughly impressed, cheered wildly as Mr Majeika finished another lap of the field, with Trigger's teeth inches from his ankles. Clearly the dog wasn't going to let him stop.

Hoping to reach the safety of the Refreshment Tent, Mr Majeika took a running jump over one of the stalls that blocked his way – but landed in a heap in the middle of it.

It was Councillor Mrs Brace-Girdle's cake stall. Jam sponge, Dundee fruit slab, Black Forest gateau, three-tiered wedding cake, all finished up in a hideous mess, most of it spread over Mr Majeika.

P.C. Bobby managed to catch Trigger. Presumably the magic had worn off, for Trigger immediately fell into a contented sleep once more.

'Well, everyone,' announced Mr Potter, 'that was a triumph, wasn't it!'

Councillor Mrs Brace-Girdle was not of the same opinion. 'I told you!' she fumed, scraping her best cakes off Mr Majeika. 'That man should never have been let near Much Barty.'

Even Mr Majeika's energy had begun to flag a little after the dog-chase. 'How am I doing?' he muttered, as Thomas and Melanie fetched him a cool drink and fanned him with their jerseys. 'Do you think I stand a chance?'

'Best Bartyan? Well, you certainly ought to be in the

running by now,' said Melanie. 'Though Mummy's cake stall may be a black mark against you.'

'And now,' announced the voice of Mr Potter over the loudspeakers, 'we come to *the* highlight of this afternoon's pot-pourri. The final event!' (To which he added, out of earshot of the microphone, 'Thank goodness!') 'I am of course referring to this year's Queen of the Fête Float, for which this year Councillor Mrs Brace-Girdle has chosen the theme "Sprites of Summer". Even now I can see the good ladies of Much Barty, with Mrs Pamela Bigmore as this year's Queen, already aboard their float on the other side of the field, next to the duck pond, ready to be drawn across to delight our eyes with their charm and beauty. Ladies, we welcome you!'

There was some clapping, and a few rude remarks by some locals who thought the Queen of the Fête Float was the silliest event each year. However, the float itself didn't move.

Mr Potter shaded his eyes with his hand and peered across the field. 'Having a little trouble, ladies?' he called through the microphone.

Thomas and Melanie could see Melanie's mother waving frantically at Mr Potter.

'What's that?' called Mr Potter. 'There's no one to drive the tractor? Oh dear.'

'I'll do it!' It was Mr Majeika of course, leaping to his feet once more.

'But you've no idea how to drive a tractor, have you?' said Thomas.

'Come and show me,' said Mr Majeika, and together they ran across the field.

The Sprites of Summer were looking rather chilly in their costumes; each of them was holding a cardboard cut-out sun, but the day was by now far from sunny. 'Do get a move on!' snapped Pam Bigmore, 'we're all freezing. Why weren't you here before?'

'It's not supposed to be him at all,' explained Thomas. 'The real driver has gone missing.' But Pam Bigmore showed no gratitude that Mr Majeika was saving her show.

'Get into the driving seat,' Thomas explained to Mr Majeika, 'turn that key to start the engine, use that lever to put it into gear, then manage the pedals as best you can. Good luck!'

Mr Majeika started the tractor and revved it up. 'It seems to be quite easy,' he called to Thomas.

'Thank you, Mr Majeika,' Mr Potter announced into the microphone. 'And here they come at last, the Sprites of Summer, with Mrs Bigmore looking especially *ravissante*, and haven't the village hall curtains adapted well to make those lovely costumes?'

But Mr Potter, his head buried in his notes, was not watching. The Sprites of Summer had not moved at all. The tractor jerked unsteadily forward and began to wobble across the field towards the crowd, but no one had remembered to check the bar that fastened it to the float, the pin of which had come adrift the moment Mr Majeika moved off. The Sprites stood, abandoned, on their float.

'You've left them behind!' shouted Thomas to Mr Majeika as he ran alongside the tractor.

Worse was in store. Deprived of its coupling to the tractor, the float acted like a see-saw. The back end, heavy with Sprites, tipped sharply down to the ground, throwing the Sprites off backwards – straight into the duck pond!

'Well, well!' called Mr Potter. 'Mrs Brace-Girdle has really surpassed herself this year. What an ingenious idea, Swimming Sprites! What a naughtily nautical twist! Isn't that nice!'

Certainly the crowd greatly appreciated the sight of muddy Sprites, tangled with duckweed, attempting to get themselves out of the pond – and none muddier than Pam Bigmore. 'Better 'n last year, Mr Potter,' observed an old man with a long white beard. 'Much better 'n last year!'

Councillor Mrs Brace-Girdle was not of the same opinion. 'This is the final outrage! That *tramp*, that person Majeika, has deliberately ruined the entire afternoon from start to finish!'

But it was not the final outrage. The final outrage was still to come. Thomas had told Mr Majeika how to *start* the tractor, but he hadn't told him how to *stop* it. He could see Mr Majeika trying all the levers one after the other, and he called out: 'Put your foot on the footbrake!'

It was too late. The tractor, scattering the crowd to both sides, careered through the platform on which stood Mr Potter's microphone, and disappeared into the Refreshment Tent.

Thomas could not bear to look. He shut his eyes. When he opened them, the Refreshment Tent had collapsed on top of the tractor in an untidy heap.

'Oh no!' he said. 'So much for poor Mr Majeika's chance of being Best Bartyan.'

'Wait a minute,' said Melanie. 'Something's happening!' The tent was magically re-erecting itself.

In a moment everything was back to normal.

'Well!' breathed Thomas, 'I've said it before, and I'll say it again. He's magical, Melanie!'

Mr Majeika walked rather sheepishly out of the tent. He was carrying the Best Bartyan Cup. 'I thought I ought to rescue this,' he said to Mr Potter. The cup was rather badly bent.

'Oh dear,' said Melanie. 'Mummy will be even crosser with him. She won't want a bent cup sitting on her mantelpiece when she wins it this year.'

'I suppose she *will* win it now,' said Thomas gloomily.

'Bound to. There's nothing we can do about it.'

'Attention, everyone!' called Mr Potter. 'Before we all go home, I call upon our guest of honour, Earl Barty, to present – and it's in his gift, of course – our trophy for the Best Bartyan.'

The spectators gathered round.

'What does he mean, "it's in his gift"?' Thomas asked.

'The Earl himself chooses who's going to get the cup,' said Melanie. 'Not that there's much doubt. Mummy's been a friend of his for years.'

And indeed it was once again Mrs Brace-Girdle who wheeled Earl Barty up to the microphone. The old man seemed to be asleep. Mr Potter nudged him awake, and set up the microphone by his wheelchair.

'Errmm,' said Earl Barty, stirring from his deep slumber. 'Ah yes. We meet today, on this auspicious field of battle, to choose a hero, a hero from among heroes.' He seemed to be falling asleep again. 'This Sceptr'd Isle, this Albion, many a hero has it produced. Winnie the Churchill . . . Winnie the Pooh . . .' He nodded off once again; Mr Potter woke him. 'But never, in the whole history of Much Barty, has so much been owed, by so many, to . . .' And once more the old man drifted into sleep.

'Do you think he's talking about Mr Majeika?' asked Thomas hopefully.

'Not a chance,' said Melanie. 'He's just saying anything that comes into his head. Mummy says that the only thing that ever wakes him up is a large whisky and soda.'

Suddenly Earl Barty jerked awake. 'Large whisky and soda?' he said loudly. 'Large whisky and soda, did someone say? Oh, most certainly, thank you, and go easy on the soda.'

Mr Potter looked around confusedly. 'I'm afraid we don't have such a thing here. If you'd care to come back to my residence afterwards, Your Lordship, I have some excellent brown sherry . . .'

'I gave you a cup of tea,' Councillor Mrs Brace-Girdle was saying crossly to the Earl. 'And it's only four o'clock. Now do get on and award that cup to me.'

'Tea! Tea!' muttered the Earl. 'Always blessed *tea* on these occasions. Can't you sometimes, Bunty, think of other people? You haven't changed a bit, have you? You were always a selfish little girl, and now you're a thoroughly selfish woman. Tea, indeed!'

'Would this be any use?' said a voice. It was Mr Majeika. Melanie and Thomas had noticed his hair twitching, and now he stepped forward, holding the Best Bartyan Cup.

'Eh, what?' spluttered the Earl. Then he looked into the cup and sniffed. 'Oh, I say, wherever did you get that?' He drank deeply from the cup. 'Best Highland malt whisky, and not too much soda, just as I said. Well, well. Now, let's award this cup thing. Well, my dear chap, since you know how to make the best use of it, you'd better keep it.' And he handed the cup back to Mr Majeika.

'Mummy's furious,' Melanie told Mr Majeika, as they all went back to the windmill to celebrate. 'But you're pleased, aren't you?'

Mr Majeika smiled blissfully. 'It's a dream come true,' he said.

'And you scarcely cheated by using magic at all,' said Thomas. 'You deserved that cup for all your hard work. The only magic bit was when you produced that whisky out of thin air.'

'That wasn't really magic,' said Mr Majeika. 'I'd just won the whisky on the bottle stall. I only had to pour a little of it into the cup.'

'I bet Mummy will come armed with crates of whisky

next year,' said Melanie. 'She'll be determined to win the cup back from you. You will be here next year, won't you?' she added, a little worried.

'Well,' said Mr Majeika, 'who can say? With the Best Bartyan Cup on my mantelpiece, even the Worshipful Wizard should begin to regard me as a thoroughly responsible person!'

'*Another successful day, Majeika?*' said a voice in Mr Majeika's ear.

'Oh yes, sir,' answered Mr Majeika. 'Getting better all the time!'

3

BEWITCHED

Mr Potter was lonely. When Class Three and Mr Majeika, and the other children and their teachers, had gone home for the evening, St Barty's School seemed very quiet. Mr Potter missed the cheerful bustle in the passages. He missed the sound of the children chattering. He even missed – extraordinary as it seems – the shouts of Hamish Bigmore.

One night, Mr Potter sat at the open window of his study, writing an advertisement to be inserted in the Lonely Hearts column of the *Bartyshire Echo*. 'Lonely Schoolmaster,' it began, 'alone in charming village of Much Barty, seeks . . .' He thought for a moment, sucking the end of his pencil, and yawning. '. . . seeks Lady Companion, still in her prime.' His pencil broke, and he found another. 'Refinement essential. Good looks an advantage.' He stopped and thought again. That seemed to be about all. 'Apply to School Cottage, Much Barty.'

The clock struck midnight. 'Is that the right time?' he said to himself. His head began to droop, and he fell asleep at his desk.

Outside, a summer night-breeze stirred. There came a little gust of wind, and it blew in at the open study window, catching up Mr Potter's advertisement, and wafting it out of the window, away on the breeze.

The letter floated up and up through the night air, higher and higher, above Much Barty where Mr Majeika was asleep in his windmill, above the Brace-Girdle and Bigmore houses, above Thomas Grey's cottage, right above Bartyshire and into the dark regions above.

It floated as high as Walpurgis.

The Wizards of Walpurgis were sound asleep, not because it was night-time, but because the Wizards of Walpurgis were almost always asleep these days. Life in Walpurgis was very dull without Mr Majeika and his muddled spells, and the disasters he used to cause. Though the Worshipful Wizard wouldn't have liked to admit it, they all missed him.

They were snoring now, all except one: a lady wizard. In fact, not to put too fine a point on it, a witch.

A witch by the name of Wilhelmina Worlock.

As Mr Potter's advertisement floated in through the open window of the Wizards' Chamber in Walpurgis, Wilhelmina Worlock was awake and brooding. Brooding on a wrong that had been done to her in the not so distant past. Done to her by none other than Mr Majeika.

She had lost a lot of sleep since he left Walpurgis. She had sat awake, night after night, thinking about him and wondering how he was getting on in Britland.

You see, Wilhelmina Worlock was in love with Mr Majeika. She had wanted to marry him. And at the last minute, he had said 'No'.

That was thirty-nine years ago. For thirty-nine years she had been hoping he might change his mind and say 'Yes'. Sometimes he had looked as if he might say 'Yes' after all. In fact, after thirty-eight-and-a-half years, Wilhelmina Worlock had become quite convinced that he was about to say 'Yes' at the very next moment.

And then, all of a sudden, he had failed his exams yet again and been sent away to Britland. As a teacher.

Now, Wilhelmina Worlock was waiting for a sign from down below. For a sign from Britland. For a sign from a teacher in Britland that she was wanted down there, that he was lonely, and that he'd say 'Yes'.

Mr Potter's advertisement floated in front of Wilhelmina Worlock's eyes. She shot out a black-taloned hand and made a grab for it. She read it. 'Lonely Schoolmaster . . . Much Barty . . . Lady Companion . . .' Yes! This was it! The letter she had been waiting for.

She covered it with kisses, crooning, 'My Majeika!' She woke up several wizards with the noise. They were extremely cross with her. Never mind, she would leave for Britland in the morning.

Mr Majeika was pinning out his socks on the clothes-line outside the windmill when he saw the balloon. It was small, black and shiny, and it was coming down through the sky, heading straight for his windmill.

'Oh no,' he said. 'Something from Walpurgis. I must be in trouble again. Whatever it is, I don't want it!'

His hair twitched, and in a moment he had magicked quite a strong little wind. It blew the balloon off course, well out of sight of the windmill.

'Phew!' said Mr Majeika. 'A near thing.'

As it happened, the wind blew the balloon straight towards the centre of Much Barty. In fact, straight to St Barty's School: into the playground, and through the open window of Mr Potter's study.

A letter was attached to the balloon's string. Magically, the balloon deposited the letter on Mr Potter's desk, and then rose in the air and soared out of the window again, up towards Walpurgis.

Mr Potter, who was sitting at his desk eating toast and reading the newspaper, glanced up and saw the letter. 'Ah,' he said, 'post's early this morning.'

He opened the letter. As he did so, a small photograph fell from it on to the floor. Mr Potter did not notice it.

'Dear Best Beloved,' read the letter, 'delighted to get your note at last. Arriving Much Barty soonest. Your loving Wilhelmina.'

'Must be some mistake,' muttered Mr Potter, throwing the letter into the waste-paper basket and returning to his newspaper.

But he did not throw away the photograph, because he hadn't seen it. And the photograph winked to itself, and slid away under Mr Potter's study door – and in a moment the door had opened, and in the doorway stood Wilhelmina Worlock.

'Coo!' she said, 'that envelope sticky stuff don't half mess up one's hair. Still, I'm here now, Best Beloveds!' She came forward with outstretched arms. She was very big and plump. 'Post Haste, Best Beloveds,' she crooned at Mr Potter, who was still buried in his newspaper. 'Special Delivery, my darlingest Majeika!' Mr Potter was still reading. 'Oy!' shouted Wilhelmina Worlock.

Mr Potter lowered his paper, and Wilhelmina's jaw fell.

'Oo are you?' she asked. 'You ain't my marvellous Majeika.'

Mr Potter got to his feet and held out his hand. 'I don't believe I've had the pleasure, madam,' he said. 'Dudley Potter, Headmaster.'

Miss Worlock sat down on a chair, all aghast. 'You means it wasn't my Majeika as has sent for me at last?'

Mr Potter shook his head. 'If, as I suspect, dear lady, you have come in answer to my advertisement in the Lonely Hearts column of the *Bartyshire Echo*, it was I who placed that announcement. May it be that we are fellow Lonely Hearts?'

Miss Worlock took a closer look at him. 'Well,' she said, 'it may. Would you be the 'eadmasters here?' Mr Potter nodded. 'And my Majeika, does he teach in your school?' Mr Potter nodded again. 'In that case,' said Wilhelmina, 'you'll do, for the time being.' A little romance with the headmaster would give her a chance to see what Majeika was up to, she reckoned. And the old boy didn't look so bad himself.

'Very wells, then,' she said cheerfully. 'Get the bests spare-room ready! Wilhelmina is movings in!'

'Ah,' said Mr Potter thoughtfully. 'I don't think that would be quite seemly, dear lady, not with both of us being in an unmarried condition. The Barty Arms seems to be a more appropriate perch for your dear self.'

'Some common or gardens pub?' fumed Wilhelmina. 'Listen, Mr Pottys, I'll has you know I'm used to the bests things in lifes, like staying in ten-star hotels and eating off nettle-plated plates . . .'

'Dear lady,' cooed Mr Potter, 'the Barty Arms is of the very best. Allow me to escort you there at once.'

Harry, the landlord of the Barty Arms, was dozing at his bar when Wilhelmina Worlock breezed in with Mr Potter in tow. Mr Potter introduced them.

'Well now, Hairy,' demanded Wilhelmina, 'I wants your bestest room, with a view of a nice stagnant pond, and – of course – a ten-mattressed bed!'

'Ten mattresses, madam? You got back trouble?' mumbled Harry.

''Course I ain't got back troubles, you brainless Britlander,' fumed Wilhelmina. 'All qualified witches sleeps on ten mattresses.'

Harry showed her up to his best room, which over-looked the back yard and a pile of beer crates. After a lot of grumbling, he was persuaded to find seven spare mat-tresses, rather damp and mouldy ones, which he piled on to the bed. Wilhelmina then conjured two more into place, which left Harry blinking. He went downstairs to pull himself a pint and report to his cronies on the new arrival. 'Calls 'erself a witch and, my gawsh, she bloomin' well looks like one.'

Word of the new arrival quickly spread through Much Barty, and in no time at all Thomas Grey, concerned to discover as much as he could about the newcomer, was mounting a pile of beer crates that he and Melanie had stacked outside Miss Worlock's window.

'I think I can just about see her now,' he whispered. 'Yes, she's there all right, talking to herself in the mirror, like the wicked queen in *Snow White*. Gosh, she does look a fright.'

Wilhelmina had dressed herself in a wedding veil, and had propped a framed photo of Mr Majeika by the mirror. 'I'll find you, never fears, Best Beloveds,' she told the picture. And, to herself in the mirror, she went through the Walpurgian wedding ceremony: 'Dost thou Wilhel-mina, take Majeika to be thy awful wedded wizard? Oh, I do, I do! Thirty-nine years, and now I'll be his bride at last!'

Thomas was so horrified that he fell off the beer crates. 'It's awful,' he told Melanie, as she helped him to his feet and dusted him down. 'Quite awful. She's magical and all, and she's after him.'

They went to warn Mr Majeika in his windmill (it was a Saturday morning, with no school).

'She's here,' they told him.

'Who is?' blinked Mr Majeika, who had forgotten about the Walpurgian black balloon.

'Someone who's been wanting to marry you for thirty-nine years.'

'And now she's come to be your awful wedded wife.'

Mr Majeika rose to his feet in terror. 'Oh *no*! Not Wilhelmina Worlock! Quick, we must bar the door, black out the windows, do anything to hide from her. Help me! Help me!'

Harry the landlord was in the bar gossiping about Miss Worlock when the telephone rang. It was the lady herself, phoning down from her room.

'Yes, Miss Worlock,' said Harry into the phone. 'Certainly, Miss Worlock. I'll just write it down, Miss Worlock.'

He got a bit of paper and began to write. By the end, he looked a little dazed.

'Okay, Miss Worlock, I'll see what I can do.'

'What did she want?' asked one of his cronies.

'Needs a bit of shopping done for her,' said Harry. 'Not exactly the sort of stuff you can get at the supermarket, though. Listen to this: "Two pounds of ferrets. One gross of fleas. And a cauldron."'

The cauldron had arrrived by mid-morning (Harry found it in the Merrie Britlande Antiques Shoppe on the village green) and the ferrets and fleas were acquired from the village poacher. In her bedroom, Miss Worlock stirred a mixture.

'Hair of ferrets . . . tongues of fleas . . . gums of gnus . . . winkles' knees . . .' (she had brought several items with her from Walpurgis, in her sponge-bag, just in case) '. . . *make him love the first woman he sees.*'

She wasn't taking any chances. It was the strongest love-potion she knew. And there was no need to make Mr Majeika swallow it. Simply by mixing it up in her hotel room and chanting the verse, she could get the spell to work.

'*Make him love the first woman he sees . . .*'

Councillor Mrs Bunty Brace-Girdle, in her Brown Owl uniform, was out collecting for the Brownies. Melanie and Thomas, in their Brownie and Cub Scout outfits, were (very unwillingly) accompanying her.

Mrs Brace-Girdle was thoroughly cross; she had managed to get only fifty pence from Pam Bigmore, even though Ronnie Bigmore, Hamish's father, was at home, 'and pottering about the house in all those gold bangles,' said Mrs Brace-Girdle irritably. 'Obviously the man is *made* of money, though it doesn't do to ask where he got it from.'

Her last port of call was Mr Majeika's windmill. Melanie and Thomas had tried to persuade her to leave Mr Majeika alone, as they feared trouble, knowing that he had boarded up his doors and windows against a certain person; Mrs Brace-Girdle was not likely to take kindly to that. But she insisted. 'It's time that tramp contributed something useful to the community,' she said firmly. 'He can give us a pound for the Brownies. It'll go some way towards making amends for the havoc he's caused so far.'

She marched along towards the windmill, with Melanie and Thomas hanging back a little for fear of what might happen. As they came up the lane, a small cloud passed over the sun and seemed to dive down and enter the windmill through a crack under the door. Though they did not know it, it was Miss Worlock's spell homing in on its target: '*Make him love the first woman he sees ...*'

Councillor Mrs Brace-Girdle knocked at the door.

'Go away,' said a voice.

'Now, Mr Majeika,' snapped Mrs Brace-Girdle, 'come along, open up like a good citizen. I want a nice generous donation from you for the Brownies.' She rapped at the door again.

'Oh well,' said the muffled voice, 'if it's really you . . .'

Mr Majeika opened the door.

'That's the stuff,' said Mrs Brace-Girdle, holding out the tin. 'A pound will do fine, if you have it on you. And perhaps you could find us a few pence more? The Brownies are a very worthwhile – oh!' She broke off in mid-sentence as Mr Majeika swooped forward and swept her up in his arms.

'Councillor Girdle!' he cried. 'Bunty! My own! My very dearest!'

'Take your hands off me, you tramp!'

But there was no stopping him. 'Bunty! Can't you see! I love you! Why have I never before drunk in your beauty? Bunty, be mine! Be mine!'

Mrs Brace-Girdle shook herself free and took to her heels.

Mr Majeika was not to be stopped, however.

'It's like something from a film,' breathed Thomas. 'He's chasing her round the windmill.'

'Something funny's happened,' said Melanie. 'He's not himself at all. Do you know what, Thomas?'

'Yes, Melanie, I know what you're thinking. It's quite definitely magical.'

Mrs Brace-Girdle beat an undignified retreat down the lane, while Mr Majeika, conscious that his advances were not welcomed by the lady, sat on the steps of the windmill with his head in his hands. 'My own, my beloved,' he cooed. 'And she won't even look at me.'

But his moans were interrupted by the sound of someone else shrieking in fury. It was Miss Worlock. She had just bustled up the lane and run smack into Mrs Brace-Girdle. 'Get out, you overblown Brownie!' she shrieked. 'What right had you to go knockings on Mr Majeika's doors? I can see what's happened, fallens for *you* he has, and not for poor Wilhelmina!'

Mr Majeika saw her. 'Aarrghh!' he cried and tried to make his escape into the windmill. But it was too late: Wilhelmina was on him, pinning him down with an arm-lock.

The two of them gazed at each other.

'Wilhelmina,' muttered Mr Majeika. 'My nightmare!'

'It's been so longs, Majeika,' crooned Miss Worlock.

'Not long enough, Wilhelmina.'

With her spare hand, she ruffled his hair. 'Remember the night we met?' she purred.

'All too well,' groaned Mr Majeika.

'You was –'

'Sick!'

'Yes, Best Beloveds, sicks with loves for me.'

'No – just sick!'

'You needs me, Majeika. You needs me in Much Bartys to be your awful wedded wife.'

'No I don't.'

'We was like Romeos and Juliets once,' Miss Worlock sighed.

'More like Laurel and Hardy,' said Mr Majeika.

Back in her hotel room, Miss Worlock put through a telephone call to Walpurgis. (Harry the landlord said it was impossible to ring another world, but Miss Worlock told him how to do it: you hold the telephone upside down.)

Once she was through, she demanded to speak to Dennis Potion, the Wizards' Apothecary, whose job it was to mix all the strange medicines and concoctions that Walpurgians require for their spells.

Dennis came on the line, and Wilhelmina fumed at him for five minutes about how useless his love-potion recipe had been.

'Hasn't been useless at all, Willy,' Dennis answered curtly. 'Not my fault if some other dame breezes up and sweeps the poor lad off his feet before he can set eyes on you. Anyway, I doubt if even *that* spell could have done the trick with Majeika. We've been through it all before, . Willy. The plain fact is that, in a hundred and thirty-nine years, Majeika would never fancy you. In fact, to be frank, he can't stand you, and he never will! Give him up, Willy, give him up!'

'I can't give up,' Wilhelmina sobbed into the phone. 'I could eats him to little pieces, I coulds. And I want him to feel the same way about mees.'

Dennis Potion sighed. 'Well, Willy, if you're that desperate – and obviously you are – there *is* one more thing we could try. Even stronger than the stuff you've used already. I'm talking about Love Potion Number Nine. I'll send a bottle down by balloon right away.'

Hamish Bigmore was coming out of the village shop with a large box of Black Magic chocolates that his mother had just bought him. He was picking out the squidgy ones and stuffing them into his mouth, and throwing the others away.

Wilhelmina Worlock, lurking on the village green with a gigantic bottle under her arm, spotted him. 'Hmm,' she said to herself. 'Black Magics! That looks promising.'

A moment later, Hamish found his arm seized by a black-taloned hand. 'Hello, my dearies,' said Wilhelmina Worlock.

'Huh?' grunted Hamish suspiciously.

'What's your name, my dearies?'

'Hamish Bigmore. And get your hands off my choccies.'

'Hamish Bigmouths, eh? Do you know who I am, Hamish?'

Hamish shrugged his shoulders and stuffed in another chocolate. 'Well, you're not a fairy princess.'

'I'm a witch, Hamish Bigmouths, a real live witch.'

'Cor!' muttered Hamish, thoroughly impressed. 'Not a real filthy black magic witch, are you?'

Miss Worlock thought about this for a moment. 'Well, a fairly dirty greys, dearies.'

'Cor!'

'I've been looking for someone like you, Hamish Bigmouths. I think you mights be just the right bad little boy for the job.'

Councillor Mrs Brace-Girdle had summoned several of her ladies to morning coffee in the Cherry Tree Tea Rooms, in order to discuss the setting up of more Committees. There was going to be a Committee to Keep Much Barty Quieter, a Committee to Make Our School Children Speak More Properly, and several other busy-body committees which no one but Mrs Brace-Girdle would have dreamt of starting. The other ladies only took part in such things because they were too scared to say 'No' to Mrs Brace-Girdle.

However, today the Much Barty ladies were showing more spirit than usual. They all thought the new Committees sounded thoroughly silly, so none of them had bothered to come to the meeting in the Cherry Tree Tea Rooms, and Mrs Brace-Girdle was left angrily sipping coffee by herself. She was still feeling thoroughly flustered after Mr Majeika's extraordinary behaviour earlier that morning; she was just thinking of setting up a Committee to Get Rid Of Mr Majeika when she saw his moon-face staring at her through the window. 'Oh no!' she said, and asked the waitress to put up the 'CLOSED' sign on the door.

But there was no stopping the love-sick Mr Majeika who was still suffering badly from the effects of Wilhelmina Worlock's spell.

'My Bunty!' he cried, and in a minute he had rushed into the Tea Rooms and thrown himself down in the chair opposite her.

'Mr Majeika!' spluttered Mrs Brace-Girdle, outraged. 'Kindly leave at once.'

'Bunty, my darling,' cried Mr Majeika, 'has anyone ever told you that your skin is like . . .' (he searched for Walpurgian terms of endearment) '. . . like a lizard's forehead? Or that your eyes are like – like two stagnant pools? And as for your pong!'

'How dare you?' fumed Mrs Brace-Girdle. 'I shall send for the police.'

Melanie and Thomas, who had been following Mr Majeika as he roamed the village looking for Mrs Brace-Girdle, having failed to persuade him to leave her alone, stood in the Tea Rooms' doorway, aghast and giggling.

'This is awful,' said Melanie. 'We must get him out of here before Mummy fetches P.C. Bobby and there's some real trouble.'

'Get out of my way,' said an unpleasant voice. It was Hamish Bigmore, clutching the most enormous spray-bottle Melanie and Thomas had ever seen.

'Who are you pushing?' said Thomas.

Behind Hamish loomed the bulk of Wilhelmina Worlock. 'Get a move on, Hamish Bigmouths,' she was whispering. 'Get in there with that love-potion, and spray him with the stuff. *Then* he'll love little Wilhelmina, you sees if he doesn't!'

Hamish and the bottle squeezed through the doorway with difficulty. 'Stop him, for goodness' sake!' muttered Melanie.

'There's no stopping Hamish,' said Thomas. 'And anyway, things couldn't get any worse than they are now.'

'Now, spray it! Spray it!' yelled Miss Worlock.

Hamish sprayed the love-potion – all over Councillor Mrs Brace-Girdle.

'You nincompoop!' screamed Wilhelmina Worlock. 'Not over *her*, over *him*!'

But it was too late. With a love-light in her eyes, Councillor Mrs Brace-Girdle rose to her feet, stretching out her arms to Mr Majeika.

'Oh, Majeika!' she crooned.

'Oh, Bunty!' crooned Mr Majeika.

'Oh, cripes!' said Thomas.

'I wonder how long it lasts?' Melanie wondered. She and Thomas had pursued Mr Majeika and Mrs Brace-Girdle as they waltzed through the village like lovers in a television commercial.

'You can almost hear the soppy music,' said Thomas.

Now the two were sitting, hand in hand, beneath the spreading chestnut tree on the edge of the village green, staring moonily into each other's eyes, and crooning, 'Oh, Bunty!' and 'Oh, Majeika!'

'We'll have to do something,' said Melanie. 'If we don't, nothing will ever stop them, and Daddy isn't going to like it a bit.'

'I shouldn't worry,' said Thomas. 'You can bet Miss Worlock is working overtime to cancel the spell.'

*

She was. She had put in another upside-down long-distance call, and she was shrieking at Dennis Potion for his uselessness.

'Me useless!' Dennis yelled back at her down the line. 'What about you? What were you doing, getting some idiotic Britland bratling to spray the stuff for you? Why ask a child? You don't *like* children, do you, Willy?'

'Oh yes I do,' grinned Wilhelmina. 'I likes 'em a lot, especially fried. But listens 'ere, Dennis, you've gots to find an antidotes to this spell, somethings that will stop the potion workings right away, do you hear?'

'Don't you give me orders, Wilhelmina Worlock, you incompetent old bats-wing,' grumbled Dennis. 'Anyway, we haven't got an antidote to this stuff.'

'I thought yous had antidotes to everythings, you silly Apothecary!'

'So we do, but the antidote to this one was borrowed thirty-nine years ago, and it hasn't been returned.'

'Borrowed? Who borrowed it?' screamed Wilhelmina.

'Who do you think? *Majeika* borrowed it – so that he'd be completely safe from you.'

'Wots!' screamed Miss Worlock, and slammed down the phone. 'Wots! I'll gets 'im yet – and I'll gets that antidote!'

Thomas, up on the beer crates again, had been listening at the window. 'Quick,' he called to Melanie. 'We must run to the windmill at once and find that antidote, if Mr Majeika's still got it.'

They were at the windmill in no time. Sure enough, there was a row of bottles on the window-sill. Melanie read off the labels: 'Antidote to Boils. Antidote to Blisters. Antidote to Bunions.'

'Hurry!' called Thomas, who was keeping watch out of the window. 'Wilhelmina's coming! She's after it, too.'

'Here we are,' said Melanie. ' "Antidote to Love". Now, off we go through the back door. We mustn't let Wilhelmina get her hands on it before we've used it.'

Mr Majeika and Councillor Mrs Brace-Girdle were still sitting under the spreading chestnut tree, blowing kisses at each other. Half the village had gathered to watch and giggle, but the two lovers were blissfully unaware of the onlookers.

It was with difficulty that Thomas struggled through the crowd and climbed the branches of the tree, clutching the bottle.

'Bunty, dearest!'

'Majeika, my honey!'

Thomas uncorked the bottle and poured the lot over them.

'Bunty, dear – oh, eh, what's happening?'

'Majeika – I mean – goodness, what am I doing here? Mr Majeika, why are you –?'

'Mrs Brace-Girdle, I am so sorry, I can't think of what came over me. Do forgive me.'

'Dear, dear,' said Mrs Brace-Girdle. 'It must have been something I ate. And I'm late for the Tidy Up The Graveyard Committee!'

They got up and hurried away, consumed with embarrassment. 'Better'n a play, that was,' said the old man with the long white beard.

'Well done, Thomas,' said Melanie. 'But what about *her*?'

Miss Worlock had come panting up to the tree too late. 'You bratlings!' she fumed at Thomas and Melanie. 'What did you wants to pour that stuffs over *him* for? Now he'll never love poor Willy!' And she slumped down in a heap.

'Do you know,' said Thomas, 'I almost feel sorry for her.'

'All I's got to look forwards to now in lifes,' snivelled Miss Worlock, 'is the Witches' Knitting Circle, and the Cauldron Cookery columns in the Sundays newspaper. A lonely life for mees.' She got out a black hankie and dabbed her eyes.

'Why be lonely, dear lady? Have you forgotten my Lonely Hearts advertisement?' It was Mr Potter.

Wilhelmina sprang to her feet. 'Why, Mr Pottys! You still here?'

'Indeed, dear lady,' dimpled Mr Potter. 'And at this very moment, in my cottage, the table is laid with tea for two. Do come and partake, and afterwards we could, how shall I put it, gaze into life's crystal ball together, if you take my meaning?'

'Delighteds, I'm sure,' crowed Wilhelmina. She waved her black hankie at Thomas and Melanie. 'Bye-bye, bratlings. And next times we meets, don't forget that you's talking to the future Mrs Pottys.'

'Oh well,' said Thomas to Melanie, 'we seem to have sorted things out quite well. We saved what could have been a very nasty situation.'

Melanie looked at the departing backs of Wilhelmina and Mr Potter. 'I'm not sure,' she said, 'that there isn't a worse one coming.'

4
THE FLIGHT OF
THE BUMBLEBEE

'But what's the matter with you?' asked Melanie.

'The – matter – with – me,' panted Mr Majeika, who looked very red in the face and was breathing heavily, 'is – that – I – feel – extremely – ill.'

Melanie sighed. She and Thomas were very worried about Mr Majeika, who was lying in his hammock at his windmill home looking absolutely terrible. His temperature had sent the thermometer right over the top, but he refused to take any of the medicines they suggested.

'It's – not – a – Britland – disease,' he panted. 'It's – Wilhelmina – who – has – done – it.'

'Miss Worlock?' asked Thomas. 'Do you mean she's put a spell on you?'

Mr Majeika shook his head, and then groaned still more because it hurt when he moved it. 'No – not a spell – she and Mr Potter – had me to supper – thirteen nights ago – and now I'm ill.'

'You think she poisoned you?' asked Melanie. 'That's terrible! What did she give you to eat?'

'Fried – Ferret – Fricassee,' panted Mr Majeika.

'Ugh!' said Thomas. 'No wonder you feel ill.'

Mr Majeika shook his head again. 'Perfectly all right in itself – quite delicious,' he said. 'Well-known Walpurgian delicacy. Mr Potter ate his all up. But she'd – put something – in my portion.'

'Oh dear,' said Melanie. 'I wonder why. Does she hate you because you wouldn't fall in love with her?'

Mr Majeika shook his head. 'Not just that,' he said. 'She's – definitely – up to – something.'

'Well, we shall see,' said Melanie. 'Meanwhile,' she went on briskly (at times she was quite like her mother, Councillor Mrs Brace-Girdle) 'meanwhile what we need to do is get you better. I do wish you'd take some aspirin.'

'I told you,' panted Mr Majeika, 'Britland medicine – no good. Can cure myself. Sure I can. Just – you – see.'

Wilhelmina Worlock wandered proudly around St Barty's School. Being engaged to be married to Mr Potter was almost as good as landing Majeika as her husband after thirty-nine years. And she'd show Majeika! She'd teach him to spurn Wilhelmina. Now that she'd got him out of the way by making him ill, she could have some real fun. She'd have all these Britlanders and their bratlings eating out of her hand. She'd make St Barty's School famous – as the Wilhelmina Worlock Academy!

Mr Potter had stuck up a notice at the school gate:

OWING TO THE SUDDEN ILLNESS OF MR MAJEIKA,
ST BARTY'S SCHOOL REQUIRES
A RELIEF TEACHER FOR CLASS THREE.
APPLY TO MR DUDLEY POTTER,
HEADMASTER.

Wilhelmina took one look at it, plucked it off the gate, and ate it. She wasn't going to have any Relief Teacher marching into the place! She'd show them what she could do!

*

'He'll make himself far worse,' said Melanie gloomily, 'really he will.'

'Whoops – he nearly fell into the fire then,' said Thomas. 'I do wish he'd be more careful.'

Mr Majeika was trying a Walpurgian remedy for his illness. 'We dance round a bonfire, and sweat it out,' he had explained to Thomas and Melanie. And now he had an enormous fire lit and was prancing round and round it in his pyjamas, chanting, 'I must get better, I must get better . . .'

'Poor chap,' Melanie said gloomily. 'You'd think that magicians could cure themselves when they got ill. But it looks as if illness in Walpurgis is even nastier than it is here. I do wish he'd try an aspirin!'

Five minutes later, Mr Majeika had collapsed into an exhausted heap. Melanie put the thermometer into his mouth to see how he was doing, but it began to melt, so she removed it hastily. 'We must get you to bed,' she said.

She and Thomas bundled him into the hammock, and managed to find some ice cubes in the refrigerator.

No sooner had they got him settled down than there was a knock at the door. It was Mr Potter.

'Ah,' said Mr Potter, 'how's the invalid, Majeika? Are you better? No, I see, no better. Dear, dear. But I came to reassure you. You mustn't worry at all about Class Three, Majeika, because we've been extremely lucky, very lucky indeed, to acquire at short notice the services, as teacher for Class Three, of a very dear friend of yours and mine, Majeika.'

'Dear friend, Mr Potter?' Mr Majeika repeated weakly from his hammock.

'Why yes,' said Mr Potter. 'None other than Wilhelmina Worlock. Miss Worlock has most generously offered to contribute her services as class teacher *in loco* . . . something or other. *In loco*, Majeika, Latin phrase meaning "in place of". In place of you, Majeika.'

'What!' said Mr Majeika, trying to rise from his hammock.

'Isn't that good news, everyone?' Mr Potter beamed at Thomas and Melanie. They looked aghast at him. 'Yes, Miss Worlock will take over Class Three for the duration of your illness.'

'Never!' cried Mr Majeika.

'There, there, Majeika,' said Mr Potter soothingly. 'I know how completely devoted you are to Class Three; but rest assured, they can come to no harm in Miss Worlock's capable . . .'

'Claws,' said Thomas.

'I must get better,' Mr Majeika gasped. 'I *must* get better!'

Miss Worlock's first lesson with Class Three was a recorder group. No one except Melanie could play the recorder properly, and the noise was appalling. When Wilhelmina called out: 'Turn over!' most people managed to knock over their music-stands, fall over their chairs, or trip over each other's feet.

'This won'ts do, bratlings,' said Miss Worlock. 'This won'ts do at all. This sorts of things won't make Wilhelmina famous in Britlands. Wilhelmina is going to have to thinks up a Plans.'

The children in Class Three were sent home from school with a note for their parents. Hamish Bigmore always threw away all notes from school, and he chucked this one in the swimming-pool, but his mother, Pam Bigmore, fished it out.

82

'Oh, I say,' she remarked to her husband, Ronnie Bigmore, who had just got back from seeing some 'business associates' in South America and was stretched out in a lounger-chair on the patio. 'Isn't this nice, Ronnie?'

'Wot?' asked Ronnie.

'It's from Hamish's new loco teacher, Miss Worlock, and guess what – she's forming an orchestra!'

'Yeah?' said Ronnie Bigmore.

'Isn't that nice, Hamish? You'll like playing in an orchestra, won't you, Hamish? 'Cause you like noise, don't you, Hamish?'

Hamish, who was amusing himself throwing marshmallows into the swimming-pool, said, 'Uh-huh.'

'So what instrument would you like Daddy and me to buy for you then, Hamish?'

Hamish thought for a moment.

'The biggest one,' he said.

A few days later, all of Class Three arrived at school with their instruments. Someone had brought a trumpet, Melanie had a violin that had belonged to her grandfather, someone else had some cymbals, and there were several clarinets and even a saxophone.

Miss Worlock was sorting them out when a great deal of noise broke out at the doorway of Class Three. Something very big was trying to get through the door. It was Hamish Bigmore, carrying a double bass and accompanied by both his parents.

The double bass was a great deal bigger than Hamish, but Pam Bigmore seemed very pleased about it. 'We've always wanted our Hamish to have the best of everything, Miss Worlock,' Pam explained. 'Haven't we, Ronnie?'

Hamish's father, who was helping to carry the double bass, said, 'Yeah.'

'So when he asked us for a . . .' Pam looked vaguely at the double bass, unable to remember what it was called.

'A big, um, er, thing,' said Wilhelmina, who had no idea of its name either.

'Naturally we got on the phone to Harrods right away and had one sent down for him. Didn't we, Ronnie?'

'Yeah,' said Hamish's father.

''Course you dids,' said Wilhelmina cheerily.

Hamish shoved the double bass into the middle of the classroom. 'Look at me, everyone! 'S'me! I've got the biggest instrument!' He dropped it carelessly against one of the desks.

'Oy,' said Ronnie Bigmore, taking notice for the first time. 'Careful with that, 'Amish. That costa lotta notes.'

''S'mine now,' crowed Hamish, 'and I can do what I like with it, can't I, Miss Worlock?'

''Course you cans, Hamish,' cooed Miss Worlock. 'You just leaves him in my capable cauldron, er, hands, Mrs Bigmouths. I'll make a reals little musical star of him, you see if I don'ts!'

Eventually, the 'orchestra' got itself into some sort of order, and was ready to begin practice. Wilhelmina kept cooing over Hamish Bigmore and his double bass.

'Who's going to be Auntie Willy's little helper, eh, Hamish?'

'Cor, am I, Miss Worlock?' said Hamish.

'And help Auntie Willys?'

'Cor!' said Hamish appreciatively.

Miss Worlock patted him on the head. 'That's right,' she said. 'We'll shows that Majeika that he's not the only clever teachers round here. We'll get one over a certains sicky Wizard of the Third Class, Failed!'

She went over to her music-stand, and tapped her wand for attention.

'Now, bratlings! There are three Basicals Musical Methods. First of alls there's Doh-Ray-Me and all that rubbish. So we won't bothers with *thats*.' She chucked some sheets of music on the floor. 'Then there's some Japanese method. But we ain't Japanese, is we, bratlings? So we're chuckings that ones an' all.' She threw more paper off the stand. 'Which just leaves us – *my* method!'

'Your method, Miss Worlock?' asked Melanie.

'That's right, bratling. I calls it – the Itchy Finger Method.'

'Why?' asked Thomas.

'Whys, cheeky monkeys? I'll show you whys. 'Cause if you horrible bratlings doesn't practise your instruments in all your spare times at home, then you gets horrible itchy fingers – like this!'

She pointed her wand, and all Class Three suddenly found their fingers itching horribly – all except Hamish.

'Right, see!' warned Wilhelmina. She tapped her wand again, and the itching stopped. 'Now thens, off we goes!' And she waved her wand to start the music. 'Three, two, sevens, and –'

The noise was abominable, a screeching and groaning and growling and yowling like a million cats fighting.

'Will yous play properly!' shouted Wilhelmina above the din.

'But we don't *know* how to play yet, Miss Worlock,' called Melanie, putting down her violin. 'Most of us haven't played our instruments before.'

'Then learns them, bug eyes,' snarled Miss Worlock. 'Listen!' And she pushed her face right up against Melanie's. 'Has I got precious time to teaches you squiggles and dots? Has I got time to tell yous which buttons to press, an' all that rubbish? Has I? 'Course not. I'm here as Conductress, to get all the applauses, and collect lots of bouquets from your grateful Mummies and Daddies.

85

That's *my* jobs. *Your* jobs is to gets the notes right. So, from the tops, now, Three, two, sevens, and –'

She lifted her arms, and the terrible noise began again.

'A musical evening?' Councillor Mrs Bunty Brace-Girdle asked Mr Potter.

'Yes, with Miss Jelley as guest of honour. A reunion with her little friends she used to teach in Class Three.'

'Why, what a lovely idea, Mr Potter,' said Mrs Brace-Girdle.

'Actually, it was Miss Worlock herself who suggested it. Being of an artistic persuasion, don't you know. She proposes to call it *Some Enchanted Evening*. The music, you see, will be entirely magical, so to speak.'

'How charming,' said Mrs Brace-Girdle. The two of them were talking outside the Much Barty chemist's shop. As they spoke, the shop door opened and out came Mr Majeika, pushing a wheelbarrow full of medicines, pills and lotions. He had decided to try Britland remedies after all – *anything* that might get him back to health again before Miss Worlock took entire command of Class Three and St Barty's.

'That man!' snorted Mrs Brace-Girdle, as they watched the departing back of Mr Majeika. 'I wish he'd show a little community spirit. He's so tiresome. How unlike the splendid Miss Worlock!'

'*Everything going all right, Majeika?*' It was the voice of the Worshipful Wizard in Mr Majeika's ears.

'Well, er, not really, sir.'

'*What's the matter, Majeika?*'

'Well, sir, it's Miss Worlock.'

There was a sigh. The Worshipful Wizard had already had plenty of trouble with Miss Worlock.

'*Whatever she's up to now, Majeika,*' said the Worshipful Wizard, '*I don't want to know about it. We're delighted to see her out of Walpurgis. Keep her in Britland for as long as you can, Majeika, and do us a favour.*'

'Oh, ah, yes, sir. But what sort of action might I be allowed to take, sir?'

'*That's no business of mine, Majeika. Do what you like about her. But don't let her come hurrying back to us.*'

'I see, sir. Very well, sir. But please, sir?'

'*Yes, Majeika?*'

'May I have, well, special permission, sir, to use Walpurgian methods?'

There was silence for a moment, as the Worshipful Wizard considered the matter.

'*Entirely off the record, Majeika, and between you and me, yes, you may.*'

Mr Majeika breathed a sigh of relief.

But even Walpurgian methods required him to be in good health. He *must* get better.

'But why don't you try an aspirin?' asked Melanie for the hundredth time, after Mr Majeika had made himself even more ill by swallowing all the medicines from the Much Barty chemist's shop.

'All right,' he said weakly, taking the small white pill she was offering.

He swallowed it.

Ten minutes later he was feeling on top of the world.

'This is extraordinary, Melanie!' he said. 'You Britlanders certainly know a thing or two. In fact, it's magical, Melanie!'

When Mr Majeika got to school, he found Mr Potter in a state of high excitement.

'"There's no business like show business ..."' Mr Potter was humming to himself, as he put up a poster at the school gate:

SOME ENCHANTED EVENING
ST BARTY'S SCHOOL PRESENTS
AN ALL-STAR MUSICAL EXTRAVAGANZA
WITH MUCH BARTY'S NO. 1 TEACHER
WILHELMINA WORLOCK

'Number One teacher?' queried Mr Majeika. 'Her, Mr Potter?'

'Absolutely, Majeika. Miss Worlock's done wonders in your absence. Just listen to the little dears.'

They could hear Class Three practising their pieces for the concert, while Miss Worlock shouted and screamed at them.

'Brings tears to your eyes, doesn't it, Majeika?' said Mr Potter fondly.

'It certainly does,' said Mr Majeika.

'Now,' said Mr Potter, 'I hope you're fully recovered from your illness, Majeika, because there's a lot I want you to do. For a start, here are some more posters that need putting up around the village. Wilhelmina – that is, Miss Worlock – has written these out herself. Rather fine, don't you think?'

They were lettered in bright green paint, and they read as follows:

WILHELMINA WORLOCK PRESENTS
WILHELMINA WORLOCK AND HER ORCHESTRA
IN A
WILHELMINA WORLOCK PRODUCTION
STARRING
WILHELMINA WORLOCK

Mr Majeika looked at them and sighed. 'You can rely on me, Mr Potter,' he said sadly. He felt like stuffing all the posters into the rubbish bin, but no doubt Wilhelmina would find out, and that would make everything much worse.

'The next thing, Majeika,' said Mr Potter, 'is chairs.'

'Chairs, Mr Potter?'

'That's it, chairs. Fetch about a hundred of them from the classrooms over to the village hall, would you? We need some extra chairs, I'm expecting quite a big crowd. Then there's lights, costumes, scenery, all that sort of thing, you must do the best you can, we want it all to look absolutely tip-top. Got that, have you?'

Mr Majeika nodded sadly.

'Jolly good,' said Mr Potter. 'Well, I'm off to type the programmes. Had to borrow the Vicar's typewriter, you know. Wilhelmina said mine wouldn't print her name big enough. See you later. "There's no business like show business . . ."' And off he went, humming gaily to himself.

For hours and hours Mr Majeika worked as hard as he'd ever done, shifting chairs (a bit of magic came in handy here), running up and down ladders checking lights (he didn't understand Britland electricity at all, and everything he plugged in and switched on tended to explode), putting up mirrors in the village hall dressing-room (so that Wilhelmina could admire herself in them), and finally, when Saturday came, running round the village sticking labels saying TONIGHT! on all the posters.

Meanwhile, in her room at the Barty Arms, every evening Wilhelmina paraded in front of the full-length mirror, admiring her costume for the concert – a black tutu, decorated in diamanté with little silver spiders and flies – and practising her make-up; she had bought a box of 'Evening Warts' especially for the occasion. She was going to look very remarkable indeed.

At home, Class Three practised their instruments for hour after hour. They had to, otherwise their fingers began to itch. All except Hamish Bigmore, who lay in a deckchair beside his family's swimming-pool, tucking into a box of Black Magic (the squidgy ones) with his left hand and idly turning the pages of a comic with the other. ''S'me, I'm the star of the evening,' he explained to anyone who happened to pass by. 'I have to keep up my strength.'

An hour before the concert was due to begin, Hamish's double bass was delivered to the village hall. Hamish had ordered the rest of Class Three to carry it across from the school, but Pam Bigmore wasn't having any of that. 'You're a star,' she told her little boy lovingly, 'and stars don't have their instruments carried by rabble like that. We'll have it delivered properly.'

So the Bigmores hired the biggest delivery van in the county, and at seven o'clock prompt it rolled up to the village hall. Two men in brown overalls got out and opened the back doors. The double bass was the only thing inside.

Thomas and Melanie had arrived early for the concert, and they watched as the removal man carefully carried the double bass out of the huge van and dusted it thoroughly, before taking it up the steps of the hall.

A moment later, up swept the white Rolls with the number-plate B I G 1. 'Cripes, what's this?' said Thomas, staring at the occupants. Pam Bigmore was in a long white evening dress and Ronnie Bigmore in a white tuxedo with lots of clonky jewellery.

But best of all was Hamish. He was in full evening dress, the sort of thing conductors wear in concert halls and on television: a long black tail-coat, and a stiff white shirt-front with a white bow tie. As he climbed out of the car he saw Thomas and Melanie, bowed to them in a dignified fashion, and then spoilt the effect by sticking out his tongue.

'What's that on his head?' asked Thomas.

Melanie frowned. 'It looks like a pink rubber bathing cap,' she said. 'Does he think it's going to rain in the village hall?'

'Shut up, you!' spat Hamish, and he stamped off to the dressing-room at the back of the hall.

Pam Bigmore was looking around her hopefully. 'I'm expecting the Press,' she said grandly. 'I intend to give interviews to the TV on What It Feels Like To Be The Mother Of A Child Star. I can't see any cameras yet, haven't they arrived?'

'I think the Vicar will be here with his Instamatic,' said Melanie. 'He wants to take a picture for the parish magazine.'

'Parish magazine!' snorted Pam Bigmore. 'My little Hamish is destined for grander things than that, isn't he, Ronnie?'

'Yeah,' said Ronnie Bigmore.

Backstage, Mr Potter was fussing over the arrangements for the evening. '"Curtain up,"' he was singing excitedly to himself, '"Light the lights! We've got nothing to hit but the heights ..." Ah, Majeika, there you are. Have you checked the spotlight? It's essential that *all* the light be thrown on Wilhelmina – Miss Worlock. She's quite

91

emphatic about that. Also, we have a slight seating problem. Naturally we want our guest of honour, Miss Jelley, to have a nice seat at the front, but unfortunately the Bigmore family have booked the entire front row so that their friends will get a good view of Hamish. Between you and me,' his voice sank to a whisper, 'I didn't think they'd *got* any friends.'

At that moment, the Bigmores arrived backstage. ''S'me, everyone! 'S'me! I've arrived!' chanted a familiar voice.

Pam Bigmore swept through on her way towards the dressing-rooms, and Ronnie Bigmore followed, elbowing Mr Potter out of the way.

'*Such* a nice man,' muttered Mr Potter, who clearly thought the opposite.

'Make-up! Wardrobe!' called Pam. 'Where are you? Would you please attend to Master Hamish Bigmore! I hope he's been given the Number One dressing-room?'

Of course, there was only one dressing-room, and that was reserved for Miss Worlock; and Make-up and Wardrobe was Councillor Mrs Brace-Girdle, who had agreed to help out with a comb and a few safety-pins.

'You can take the bathing cap off now, Hamish darling,' said Pam Bigmore. Hamish removed the pink rubber cap. Underneath, his hair was all in rollers. Pam had spent hours and hours giving him a perm.

'Ah, Majeika,' panted Mr Potter, hurrying up to Mr Majeika in the wings, 'you haven't forgotten, have you, that you're fetching Miss Jelley, our guest of honour?'

'No, Mr Potter,' said Mr Majeika, 'I haven't forgotten it, because you never told me.'

'Oh well, better late than never. Off you go now, there's only thirty minutes before curtain-up.'

'Where does she live, Mr Potter?'

'Quite a distance, you know. About a couple of miles away, in the Bartyshire Home for Distressed Teachers. We had to put her there, you see, when she had her final collapse after trying to teach – well, you know who.'

'I'll go right away,' said Mr Majeika. 'You'll lend me your car?'

Mr Potter thought about this for a moment. 'No, I don't think that's necessary,' he said. 'You can go on your tricycle.'

The Home for Distressed Teachers was a pleasant building in a very quiet spot. No doubt living there had done Miss Flavia Jelley a lot of good. But when Mr Majeika found her waiting in the entrance hall, she did not look at all happy.

She was wearing a very old moth-eaten evening dress, and as she stood there she quivered all over. Mr Majeika thought that her name suited her.

'Miss Jelley?' he said, holding out his hand.

'Flavia Jelley,' she answered shakily, grasping his hand very nervously. 'There's one thing I have to ask you,' she continued in her wobbly voice. '*H-he* won't be there, w-will he?'

'He, Miss Jelley?'

'You kn-know, that t-terrible, d-diabolical . . .' Her voice tailed off.

'Hamish Bigmore, Miss Jelley?' asked Mr Majeika.

Miss Jelley gasped, and clutched her throat. 'Don't say that name!'

By the time Mr Majeika had managed to get Miss Jelley back to the village hall on his trike (she sat on the box at the back, and put her arms around his waist), Mr Potter was looking anxiously at his watch. 'Three minutes to curtain, Majeika. Get the audience settled down, will you?'

Miss Jelley teetered up to Mr Potter with outstretched hand. 'Dudley,' she said affectionately.

'Flavia, my dear.' He stroked her hand in a kindly way. 'Better, I hope?'

Miss Jelley quivered. 'No better,' she sighed.

Mr Majeika conducted her to her seat. The front row was entirely empty apart from two seats occupied by the Bigmores, so Mr Majeika sat her at the end of it, even though Pam hissed out, 'Reserved!'

'Don't leave me, Mr Majeika,' Miss Jelley quivered anxiously.

'But I must, Miss Jelley. I have my duties as Stage Manager.'

'I'm scared, Mr Majeika. Scared that . . . *you know who* . . . will . . .'

'Don't worry, Miss Jelley,' Mr Majeika reassured her. 'I'll make sure that – a *certain person* – won't come anywhere near you.'

At that moment the stage curtains were pushed apart and a familiar face stuck itself out.

'Yoo-hoo, Miss Jelley!' cried Hamish Bigmore.

Miss Jelley gave a stifled scream.

'Remember me, Miss Jelley? 'S'me, your former pupil, Hamish Bigmore.'

The scream was no longer stifled.

'Thirty seconds, everyone,' Mr Potter was saying anxiously in the wings.

Councillor Mrs Brace-Girdle had got hold of her daughter Melanie and was pinning up her hair. 'There's

94

Mummy's pretty girl,' she said through a mouthful of hairpins. Melanie glared at her.

'Well, boys and girls,' said Mr Potter, 'best of luck. Not nervous, I hope, are you? Jolly good!' (He felt for his own bottle of Nerve Pills in his pocket, unscrewed its lid and swallowed one just for luck.) 'And how smart you all look.'

A wardrobe rail of clothes suddenly parted and through it peered an appalling face. 'And what about mees, Mr Pottys?' It was Wilhelmina, trying to look cute.

Even Mr Potter reeled. 'Wilhelmina, my dear, what a sight you are! What a sight!' He glanced at his watch. 'Ready, everyone! Right, Majeika. House-lights down. Curtain up – no, I'll do that myself.' And Mr Potter began to haul away at a rope, singing cheerily to himself: '"Curtain up, light the lights! We've got nothing to hit but the heights . . ."'

Unfortunately it was the wrong rope, and the end of it got caught round Mr Majeika's foot as Mr Potter pulled it, so that 'hit the heights' was what Mr Majeika did. The next thing he knew, he found himself hanging upside down from the ceiling.

'Oh really, Majeika,' said Mr Potter crossly, 'this is no time for silly games.'

Leaving Mr Majeika suspended like a salami sausage in a delicatessen, he fought his way through the curtains and out to the front of the stage.

'Welcome, ladies and gentlemen,' he beamed at the audience.

Mr Majeika's face appeared through a gap at the top of the curtains, and everyone began to laugh. 'Help!' called Mr Majeika.

'Get yourself out of this, Majeika,' hissed Mr Potter. 'It's your own silly fault.' Mr Majeika's head disappeared, and a moment later a bump was heard as he fell to the stage.

'Welcome,' continued Mr Potter, smiling glassily at the audience, 'welcome to our little Musical Extravaganza. On our packed programme this evening we feature music to suit all tastes ... however bad ... And so, ladies and gentlemen, without further ado, will you please welcome the entire St Barty's Class Three Orchestra!'

Mr Majeika found the right cord, pulled it, and the curtains opened.

There was mayhem as Class Three rushed on stage, nearly knocking Mr Potter over.

Hamish Bigmore fought for the centre of the stage and won it. ''S'me!' he called out to Miss Jelley. ''S'me! 'S'me, Miss Jelley!'

Miss Jelley, nearly fainting, was comforted by the Vicar.

Knowing the sort of trick that Wilhelmina might get up to, Mr Majeika decided to creep on stage himself and hide at the back of the orchestra.

But Wilhelmina, waiting in the wings, had spotted him, and she grabbed him in her strong claws. 'Well, well, Best Beloveds,' she cooed. 'Trying to spoil Willy's little shows, are you?' She backed him against a large cupboard and opened the door. 'Sorry, Best Beloveds, but there's only rooms for *one* Magical Megastar around heres. And that's mees, Best Beloveds!' And she shoved Mr Majeika inside the cupboard and locked the door.

'And now, ladies and gentlemen,' called out Mr Potter, 'our Conductress for the evening, Miss Wilhelmina Worlock!'

There was a burst of applause, and some rude shouts from the village lads at the back of the hall. Wilhelmina walked on and waved her wand cheerily at the audience. 'Wotcha!' she cried.

'Miss Worlock,' continued Mr Potter, studying his notes, which were all upside down, 'will now conduct the children in . . . er . . . something . . . in the renowned, er, "Plight of the Fumblebee", er sorry, "Bum of the Flightle-bee".' There was a giggle from the audience, and Miss Worlock glared at him. 'I mean,' said Mr Potter apologetically, '"Flight of the Bumblebee".' He stumbled off the stage backwards, mopping his brow.

Hamish was ready at his double bass. Or rather, at the bottom half of his double bass. It was his job to work the bow, but he had found it impossible to reach up to the top part of the strings, so Thomas had been told to stand on a chair and put his fingers on the strings for Hamish. Thomas badly wanted to muck the whole thing up and make Hamish play the wrong notes, but Miss Worlock's Itchy Finger Method made that impossible. He had to play it right – or else!

'Over here, spotlight!' Hamish called out, because the light was not shining in his direction. 'Spotlight – over here, spotlight! 'S'me, spotlight, 's'me!'

Miss Jelley stuffed a handkerchief into her mouth.

Mr Potter wondered why Mr Majeika was not working the spotlight. He looked around but could not see Mr Majeika anywhere. The fellow must have wandered off; it was very annoying. Also, something was banging about and shouting in the big cupboard in the wings.

'Do be quiet in there,' Mr Potter called in the direction of the cupboard. 'You know there's a concert in progress.'

In the cupboard, Mr Majeika sighed and scratched his head and wondered what on earth to do.

'Nows,' said Wilhelmina Worlock, tapping her wand on the music-stand like a conductor's baton, 'off we go, bratlings! Three, two, sevens, and –'

The music began – if you could call it music. It was the most hideous sound ever heard in the Much Barty Village

97

Hall, even counting the occasion when Mr Potter had tried to play 'Rudolf the Red-Nosed Reindeer' on his hand-bells one Christmas and one of the clappers had flown off and hit the Vicar on the nose.

The noise of Wilhelmina's orchestra reduced Miss Jelley, who was already in a pretty bad state, to a quivering wreck. Pam Bigmore, trying to be impressed by her son's performance, could not help stuffing her fingers in her ears. Even Ronnie Bigmore looked stunned.

'You'd never think they'd only been practising a few weeks, would yous?' Wilhelmina called out cheerily to the audience above the racket.

'I wouldn't think they'd been practising at all,' muttered the Vicar.

Over the din, a terrible howling began. At the request of Mr Potter, P.C. Bobby had been guarding the door of the Village Hall. 'It's a celebrity concert, you know,' Mr Potter had told the Constable, 'so the police ought to be in attendance to guard the VIPs.' Now P.C. Bobby's dog Trigger found the noise of the orchestra altogether too much. Trigger put back his head and howled for all he was worth.

And over the din, Hamish Bigmore, sawing away on his double bass, called out triumphantly to his mother: ''S'me, Mummy! Look at me! It's me now! 'S'me!'

Mr Majeika could not get the cupboard door to budge.

'*Everything all right, Majeika?*' said a voice in his ear. It was the Worshipful Wizard – the first time Mr Majeika had heard from him for ages.

'Desperate measures needed, I think, sir,' muttered Mr Majeika, tugging at the door. 'You did say that Walpurgian tactics might be allowed?'

'*Off the record, and quite unofficially, I think I might turn a blind eye to it, just this once.*'

'Right-oh, sir, and what do you suggest, sir? Any particular spell?'

'*That's your job, Majeika. Now's your chance to prove that you're a real wizard, and of the first class too. Now, get on with it!*'

Mr Majeika thought for a moment, and then a smile crossed his face.

A second or two later, something emerged from the keyhole of the cupboard and flew towards the stage. It was a large bumblebee.

'The Flight of the Bumblebee' was still in progress. That is, Wilhelmina was still waving her arms, and Class Three were still making noises on their instruments, though any pretence that it was music had long since ceased.

Several of the audience had demanded to be taken to hospital; they said their hearing would never recover. The only person still enjoying herself was an entirely deaf old lady who kept saying, 'When is it going to start?'

It was Thomas, working the strings of the double bass, who first spotted the bumblebee. It was a particularly large bee; but it was only when it settled on Hamish's nose and *winked* at Thomas that Thomas guessed what was going on.

'It's Mr Majeika!' he called out to Melanie above the din.

'What is?'

'The bumblebee. He's magical, Melanie!'

The bee was still on Hamish's nose, and Hamish didn't like it all. He stopped playing and began jigging about, waving his arms at the bee to shoo it away. The bee stayed put.

'What's the matter, Bigmouths?' called Wilhelmina crossly.

'There's a bumblebee on my nose, Miss Worlock!'

'I don't care if you've got a rhinoceros on your noses, Bigmouths,' snapped Miss Worlock. 'Keep playing!'

Hamish kept on thrashing about, but the bee would not budge.

Thomas laughed so much that he almost fell off his stool.

Hamish began to scream.

'Now what?' called Wilhelmina furiously.

'It's dive-bombing me!' And indeed the bee was zooming in on Hamish's face.

'Wait a minute,' snapped Miss Worlock, putting down her wand. 'Let's have a looks, Bigmouths.' She peered at the bee. 'I thoughts so! So that's your little game, eh, Best Beloveds?' She picked up her wand again and waved it in the air.

It changed into a fly-swat.

Chaos broke out as Wilhelmina started to chase the bumblebee around the stage. She fell over music-stands and crashed into the double bass, but the only thing she succeeded in hitting with the fly-swat was the end of Hamish Bigmore's nose.

'Ooooooooo!' screeched Hamish.

'My baby!' cried Pam Bigmore. 'She's hurting my baby!'

Mr Potter, watching from the wings, chewed his fingers and swallowed half a dozen Nerve Pills.

'Stop her, Ronnie!' Pam was screaming. 'Stop her thumping my little baby!'

Ronnie Bigmore, goaded into action, climbed slowly up on to the stage and picked up the double bass, holding it as if it was a gigantic fly-swat. 'Watch it, you,' he said to Miss Worlock, waving it above her head.

Wilhelmina, paying no attention, chased Hamish and the bee into the wings. 'Come on, the bee!' cried a voice. 'Come on, the bee! Three cheers for the bee!' It was Miss

Flavia Jelley, bouncing up and down in her seat like a football supporter at the Cup Final.

Mr Potter edged on to the stage, clutching his handbells. 'I'm afraid we appear to have a slight hitch with "The Flight of the Bumblebee", ladies and gentlemen,' he announced, 'but in the meanwhile I'd like to play you a selection of Christmas carols.' He began to ring his bells, but a moment later was knocked sprawling by Hamish and Miss Warlock, still engaged in their furious chase.

'I'll teach yous!' Wilhelmina was screaming at the bumblebee. 'I'll teach yous, Best Beloveds! You can't make a monkey out of me!'

'Oh, can't I?' said Mr Majeika's voice.

And Wilhelmina Worlock turned into a chimpanzee.

'Magical, Melanie, magical!' laughed Thomas helplessly as the two of them watched the chimpanzee, still armed with the fly-swat, stagger about the stage, taking swipes at Hamish Bigmore's nose.

Mr Majeika turned back into himself. 'Curtain, Majeika, curtain!' Mr Potter ordered, and the curtains closed, bringing to an end a performance that Much Barty would never forget.

Pam Bigmore came to rescue Hamish. 'There, there, darling,' she cooed, leading him off to the Rolls-Royce. 'You'll always be Mummy's little star, won't he, Ronnie?'

''Ere,' said Ronnie Bigmore to the two men with the removal van, 'you can 'ave this.' And he threw them the double bass.

'I'm giving up music, Mummy,' said Hamish, as Ronnie drove them off in the Rolls.

''Course you are, darling,' said Pam cheerily. 'Shall Daddy buy you a nice little pony instead?'

*

'Well, what an interesting evening that turned out to be, Wilhelmina,' said Mr Majeika.

Alongside him, still clutching its fly-swat, ambled the chimpanzee.

'I do hope you enjoyed yourself as much as I did,' said Mr Majeika.

The chimpanzee hit him with the fly-swat.

By the time Melanie and Thomas reached the windmill, Mr Majeika had relented and had changed Wilhelmina back into herself.

'How coulds you?' She was sobbing into her black handkerchief. 'How coulds you do that to mees, Best Beloveds? How coulds you spoil my marvellous moments of musical mellifluousnesses? I means,' and she dabbed her eyes, 'I couldn't even go on and take my bows, coulds I? Not looking like thats! How coulds you be so means to poor little Willys?'

'Never mind, Wilhelmina,' said Mr Majeika, putting on the kettle.

'Give mees another chance, Best Beloveds,' coaxed Wilhelmina. 'Leave mees alone, and let mees be a Megastar another evening. I'll get Pottys to book the village hall straight aways, shall I? And mees and Hamish Bigmouths shall do a concerts together, just a little duets. Please, Best Beloveds?' she cajoled.

'Nope,' said Mr Majeika.

'Pretty please . . .'

Mr Majeika shook his head. All of a sudden Wilhelmina bounded out of her chair and grabbed him by the shoulders. 'Pretty please, Best Beloveds, or I'll pull your hair!'

'Nope,' said Mr Majeika, struggling beneath her bulk.

'You know,' said Wilhelmina, changing to a wheedling

tone once more and settling back into her chair, 'you was very, very goods as a bumblebees, Best Beloveds.'

'Really?' said Mr Majeika, looking pleased with himself.

'Very goods. You really got me buzzing, Best Beloveds!'

'Oh, it was nothing,' Mr Majeika smiled modestly.

'Could you do it again, Best Beloveds, just for Auntie Willy?'

'Well, I don't see why not.' And Mr Majeika turned himself into the bumblebee.

'Now, Best Beloveds,' cooed Wilhelmina, 'just come over heres, sweetie-pie, on the table, that's right. Aren't you a clever little Wizard, then? You can change yourself into a bee any time you like, can't you? And guess wots! I can change into sticky flypaper any time toos, Best Beloveds!'

In an instant, Wilhelmina had become a long, sticky strip of flypaper, flapping across the room towards him. 'I'm going to squidges and squelches you alls up, Best Beloveds,' her voice cooed. 'You're nevers going to flys again, not nevers!'

The flypaper wriggled all round Mr Majeika getting closer and closer.

Thomas and Melanie looked at each other. 'This is terrible!' said Thomas. 'She'll kill him!'

'Quick!' cried Melanie. 'Roll her up!'

They made a dive for the flypaper and squashed it into a nasty sticky ball before it had a chance to trap the bumblebee.

'Ugh!' said Thomas. 'Isn't it horrible. But she won't be able to get out of this one again in a hurry.'

'No, she won't,' said Mr Majeika, reappearing as himself. He took an envelope from the table. 'Quick,' he said, 'shove her in here! Well done, you two. I was taking a chance that you'd know what to do. I knew she'd never be able to resist that old flypaper gag, and I was pretty sure you'd have the sense to bundle her up. Now,' and he began to write on the envelope, 'I think we've had quite enough of her for the present in Much Barty.'

On the envelope he wrote: 'To the Head of Spells, Walpurgis. Do NOT return to sender.'

He, Thomas and Melanie sent it off by balloon.

'*Crisis over, Majeika?*' said a voice in Mr Majeika's ear.

'Yes, sir, thank you, sir. Everything back to normal.'

'*You did very well, Majeika, very well indeed. Distinctly a First Class result. We'd better take another look at those "O"-Level papers. Perhaps they weren't so bad after all . . .*'

5

IF YOU GO DOWN TO THE WOODS TODAY

'It's no good complaining, Melanie,' said Thomas. 'You can't expect magical things to happen every day. Remember that he's not supposed to behave like a Walpurgian at all.'

'I know,' sighed Melanie, swinging her legs from the top of the five-barred gate where they sat. 'But I did expect some more fun and games after that musical evening. You know, people turning into bumblebees and chimpanzees and all that sort of thing. And nothing like that has happened for weeks and weeks. He's becoming just another ordinary schoolteacher, really he is.'

'Well,' said Thomas thoughtfully, 'there's the Scout Camp next week, when we all have to be Brownies and Cubs and all that sort of thing. He's coming on the Camp, I heard him talking to Mr Potter about it. I expect something funny will happen then.'

'I can't think what,' said Melanie. 'Scout Camp is awful. You just trudge out to the woods and have to put up tents, and it always rains, and Mummy is more bossy than ever.' (Councillor Mrs Brace-Girdle, Melanie's mother, was the Brown Owl of the Much Barty Brownie pack.) 'Even Mr Majeika couldn't make a Scout Camp exciting.'

*

'Been camping before, have you, Majeika?' asked Mr Potter, examining Mr Majeika's strange costume as the Brownies and Cubs gathered at the school on the morning the Scout Camp was to begin.

'I don't think so, Mr Potter,' said Mr Majeika doubtfully. He was beginning to wonder whether he hadn't overdone the scouting outfit a bit.

'When in Britland,' his Instruction Book said firmly, 'do as the Britlanders do, and don't do it half-heartedly.' Mr Majeika had tried to observe this when getting ready for the Camp. Mr Potter had provided him with a Scout hat, and had explained that the important thing with scouting was to Be Prepared.

'Be prepared for anything, Majeika. For dangerous wild beasts, for forest fires, for avalanches, earthquakes and snowstorms. The good Scout is never at a loss in an emergency.'

'Right you are, Mr Potter,' Mr Majeika had answered, though privately he wondered whether wild beasts, avalanches, earthquakes and snowstorms were very likely in the Bartyshire countryside in June. But he had tried to Be Prepared in every possible way, which is why he arrived at school, on the day the Camp was to begin, with all kinds of objects tied around his waist, and to his hat. There was a spade, a pick-axe, a fork, several pots and pans, firelighters and paraffin to help light a camp-fire, all the maps he could find, and his bedding. They all made rather a noise as he walked. In fact, walking was not at all easy.

'Very pleased to see you're putting so much effort into this, Majeika,' said Mr Potter. 'You'll really enjoy camping, you know.'

'Oh yes?' said Mr Majeika hopefully.

'Yes indeed. There's nothing like it. The balmy breezes, the birdsong, and just that thin piece of canvas between

106

you and the stars. Ever slept under the stars before, have you, Majeika?'

'Not exactly, Mr Potter,' said Mr Majeika, thinking of his life in Walpurgis. 'Danced under them, I have, but never . . .'

'Oh, you'll love it, Majeika, you'll love it.'

At this moment up bustled Brown Owl Brace-Girdle. 'Ah, Bunty,' said Mr Potter cheerfully. 'All ready for the fray?'

Mrs Brace-Girdle cast a doubtful glance at Mr Majeika, half hidden behind his battery of garden tools and other camping equipment. '*He's* not coming, I hope?' she said acidly.

'Mr Majeika has kindly offered to join us for the Camp as an Honorary Scout,' explained Mr Potter smoothly. 'Now, boys and girls, let's be on our way! Have you counted heads, Brown Owl?'

'Just one Cub missing, Mr Potter,' said Mrs Brace-Girdle.

'Don't tell me,' said Mr Potter. 'I can guess who.'

At that moment, around the corner came a white Rolls-Royce with the number-plate B I G 1. Pam Bigmore climbed out and opened the passenger door.

'Ah,' said Mr Potter, 'the late Hamish Bigmore.'

Out of the Rolls climbed Hamish, looking very un-enthusiastic about the Scout Camp, despite the brand-new knapsack on his back, and the brand-new bicycle that his mother was unclipping from the back of the Rolls.

'You will look after my beautiful baby, won't you, Mr Majeika?' cooed Pam.

'Of course we will, Mrs Bigmore,' he reassured her.

'And give him a nice comfy bed?'

'It won't be quite the Ritz Hotel, Mrs Bigmore,' observed Mr Potter. 'The idea is to toughen them all up a little, you know.'

Pam Bigmore gave a little shriek. 'But you will see he's tucked in properly at night, won't you? I don't want him catching a chill on his little chest.' She turned to Brown Owl Brace-Girdle. 'And he's very fussy about his din-dins, Bunty. He has everything freshly prepared. On a tray. He won't eat just anything, you know.'

(Hamish was at that moment engaged in stealing some half-eaten and rather grubby salt-and-vinegar crisps from Thomas Grey.)

'He'll eat anything if *I'm* cooking, Pamela,' observed Mrs Brace-Girdle grimly.

'Now then, everybody, off we all go!' Mr Potter called out.

'I want to lead,' sulked Hamish, as he climbed on to his bike. 'I always go first.'

'Let him go in front, Thomas,' said Melanie. 'It'll give us a bit of peace and quiet.'

'Last kissy for Mummy, Hamish darling!' called Pam Bigmore, as the procession of bicycles began to wend their way out of sight.

Last but one, on an ancient black bicycle with a big basket, pedalled Mr Potter, singing happily to himself: '"I love to go a-wandering, Along the mountain track . . ."'

And last of all, on his Walpurgian tricycle, came Mr Majeika, puffing as he pedalled up the hill, and wondering what he had let himself in for.

Class Three reached the field that had been chosen for the camp site quite quickly, but the grown-ups took a good deal longer, puffing and panting up the hills on their machines. Mr Majeika was delayed even more when Hamish Bigmore got off his bicycle and announced that he had tired legs and must be given a lift. It took Mr

Majeika almost an hour to coax him all the way to the camp site under his own pedal power.

'Well,' said Mr Potter, looking around cheerfully, 'so far it's an improvement on last year. No thunderstorm. No wasp stings. No visit to hospital. No pop festival occupying our camp site.'

They began to unpack. Everyone helped to put up a tent. 'You can have this one to yourself, Majeika,' said Mr Potter, handing over a large brown bundle. 'I expect you can manage to sort it out.'

Mr Majeika spent twenty minutes unpacking it and trying to work out which bit went where. At last he thought he had got the hang of it. 'Is this right?' he asked, walking over to where Mr Potter was supervising the others.

Mr Potter stared. 'But you're supposed to *sleep* in it, Majeika, not *wear* it!'

Melanie and Thomas giggled helplessly. Mr Majeika had draped his tent over his shoulders like some outsize dress or cloak.

'I'll help you,' said Melanie.

'Well,' said Thomas, 'someone's done all right for himself, hasn't he?' He pointed to where Hamish Bigmore, outside a gleaming new tent of his own, was relaxing on an inflatable li-lo, wearing Walkman headphones, reading a lurid science-fiction comic, and watching his own personal TV set.

With a contented sigh, Hamish reached for a handful of squidgy ones from his three-pound box of Black Magic. 'Nothing like the open-air life!' he called out cheerily.

'I wouldn't particularly mind,' said Thomas, 'if he hadn't made me put the tent up for him.'

That evening, Hamish met his match. Mr Potter had

dropped off to sleep after his exertions on the bicycle, but Brown Owl Brace-Girdle had spent the afternoon energetically organizing games in the field next to the camp site, and she soon woke Mr Potter with her cry of 'Camp-fire! Time to light the camp-fire, everyone!'

Mr Majeika and Class Three hurried off to the woods, under the supervision of Mrs Brace-Girdle, to gather wood for the fire. All of Class Three, that is, except one.

'Hamish Bigmore, what *are* you doing?' snapped Mrs Brace-Girdle, who had not noticed Hamish's absence from the games during the afternoon. 'Get off that li-lo, turn off that television, put away those chocolates, and run after the others to gather kindling for the fire.'

Hamish paid no attention to her.

'Hamish Bigmore,' repeated Mrs Brace-Girdle, 'did you hear me?'

'I'm busy,' mumbled Hamish, switching channels on the TV. 'Let the other Cubs do it.'

Mrs Brace-Girdle started to walk towards him menacingly. Hamish glanced up, saw the look on her face, dropped his comic, and tore off into the woods.

Five minutes later he was back again, carrying an armful of wood like the others, but looking thoroughly frightened.

'You look a bit pale, Hamish,' said Mr Majeika. 'Something wrong?'

Hamish bit his lip and said nothing.

The fire was lit and eventually Mrs Brace-Girdle handed round camp-fire-cooked sausages.

'I suppose you had better have one,' she said grudgingly to Mr Majeika, 'though I hadn't catered for you.'

Mr Majeika eyed the burnt sausage, dripping with grease. What extraordinary things these Britlanders did eat!

'No, thank you, Mrs Brace-Girdle,' he said politely.

'Oh,' said Mrs Brace-Girdle, displeased at her offer being refused. 'Vegetarian, are you, Mr Majeika?'

'No, Walpurgian.'

Mrs Brace-Girdle frowned and turned to Hamish Bigmore. 'Din-dins, Hamish! Sorry it's not on a tray,' she said icily.

Hamish shook his head and looked away.

'Not hungry?' Mrs Brace-Girdle asked. 'Too many choccies?'

Hamish didn't reply.

'It's not like him,' whispered Melanie. 'He usually stuffs himself with school food even straight after he's been eating sweets, the greedy pig. Do you think he saw something in the wood that frightened him?'

'Mrs Brace-Girdle says there's a legend about that wood,' said Mr Majeika to Thomas and Melanie. 'She says it's known as the Wailing Wood, because there's supposed to be a Lost Soul wandering about in there and that sometimes it wails to itself.'

Thomas shrugged. 'I should think it *would* wail if it saw Hamish Bigmore.'

There really was something in the wood. Hamish had come across it, staring at him through the branches; when he saw it, he had turned pale and run back to the camp site.

And now it was crouching at the edge of the wood, watching the campers as they got ready to go to bed. Breathing heavily, it peered at them through the long grass.

No sooner had Mr Majeika got into bed than his tent collapsed on him. Melanie helped him to put it up again, and he snuggled back into his sleeping-bag.

Brown Owl Brace-Girdle went around to tuck them all up. 'I expect we're all missing our mummies kissing us night-night tonight, aren't we? So I'll do it instead.'

She tried to kiss Thomas, but he pretended to have a coughing fit, and rolled out of her reach in his sleeping-bag. When she turned to Hamish, he had disappeared completely to the bottom of *his* bag. Tucked up in his own tent, Mr Potter wondered anxiously if the good-night kiss would be offered to him, too.

'Good-night, everyone!' he called. 'I'll sing you to sleep.' And he cleared his throat and began:

> *'Good-night, Brownies!*
> *Good-night, Cub Scouts!*
> *Good-night, Brown Owl!*
> *We're going to sleepies now.'*

'All together, sing along with me!' Mr Potter called. But everyone pretended to be fast asleep.

Mr Majeika tossed and turned, and soon his tent fell down on him again. Melanie and Thomas, who had heard the noise, wriggled out of their sleeping-bags and went to see what was the matter.

'It's no good,' whispered Mr Majeika. 'No Walpurgian can sleep under two sticks and a hankie.'

'We couldn't get to sleep either,' said Melanie. 'Not with Mummy snoring so.'

'I've brought my hammock,' said Mr Majeika. 'I'm going over to the woods to sling it there, then I'm bound to get to sleep. See you in the morning!'

'Can't we come too?' whispered Thomas.

'But you haven't got hammocks.'

'Oh, come on, Mr Majeika, be a sport. Anyway, we think Hamish Bigmore saw a ghost in the wood, and that sounds rather fun,' said Thomas.

Mr Majeika smiled. 'You don't believe in ghosts, do you?'

'Well,' said Melanie, 'we used not to believe in wizards and witches . . .'

'Come on,' said Mr Majeika, 'let's see if we can't set ourselves up comfortably for the night.'

The wood looked quite welcoming, but there were strange noises all around them: hoots and squeaks and grunts, and the rustle of leaves. 'It's only badgers and other night animals,' said Melanie to Thomas, who was looking rather nervous.

'Maybe,' said Thomas doubtfully, 'but I don't fancy sleeping on the ground. There are bound to be creepy-crawlies.'

'Well then, Thomas,' said Mr Majeika, 'we'll have to find somewhere to sleep *off* the ground. Now, that looks quite promising.' And he pointed at an enormous oak-tree in the centre of a clearing.

'How do we sleep in that?' asked Melanie. 'We'd fall off the branches.'

For answer, Mr Majeika's hair began to wiggle. Thomas and Melanie looked at each other, for they knew this meant that strange things were about to happen.

There was a rustling in the branches of the big tree, and the children saw that a platform had appeared there, out of nowhere.

'A tree-house!' breathed Thomas, but Mr Majeika motioned to him to hush.

'I haven't finished yet,' he whispered, and again his hair began to wiggle.

Thomas blinked as he watched walls, doors and windows appearing in order around the platform. In a moment, all four walls and the roof were there. The house even had a white-painted balcony at its front, and a chimney from

113

which smoke began to curl. Last of all, a rope-ladder unrolled itself from the platform down to the ground.

'Well, what do you think?' asked Mr Majeika, looking pleased with himself.

'Can we sleep in it, too?' asked Melanie, excited.

Mr Majeika nodded.

'Wow!' said Thomas. 'Now that really is magical, Melanie!'

The tree-house was even nicer inside than out. The fire in the hearth was blazing, and in a moment Mr Majeika had conjured out of nowhere a delicious supper of fish fingers, baked beans and chips, followed by iced lollies – altogether much nicer than burnt sausages.

'I oughtn't to be doing all this magic really,' said Mr Majeika sheepishly, 'but nobody except you was watching, and the Worshipful Wizard doesn't seem to mind me doing one or two Walpurgian things these days, ever since I managed to deal with Wilhelmina for him.'

They finished supper, and Thomas looked at the fire. 'The wood is burning rather low,' he said. 'Why don't we gather some more before we go to sleep?'

'All right,' said Mr Majeika. 'You and Melanie just pop out with the basket, and I'll get ready for bed.'

The children went down the rope-ladder, and Mr Majeika looked around happily. He was very pleased with the tree-house. 'Not bad for an Apprentice Wizard,' he muttered to himself.

Outside, on the edge of the clearing, Melanie and Thomas were gathering sticks, but Thomas kept looking over his shoulder uneasily. 'Melanie,' he whispered, 'don't you get the feeling there's someone else around?'

Melanie shrugged her shoulders. 'Not particularly,' she said. 'The whole forest is full of night-creatures, but I

114

don't feel specially –' She broke off. Then she said, in a whisper: 'You're right, Thomas. We're not alone!'

She motioned him to look. There, in a clump of tall grass and ferns, they could make out a pair of boots, attached to someone's legs . . . The legs of a very old man, dressed in very old clothes. Not the sort of old clothes you find at jumble sales, but in quite a different style: the kind of clothes you see worn in ancient portraits and in history books.

'Gosh!' whispered Thomas. 'Who do you think he is?'

'I don't know,' whispered Melanie. 'I think we ought to fetch Mr Majeika. I have a feeling that this is not just an ordinary tramp. In fact, he looks thoroughly Walpurgian. I bet he's the ghost that Hamish saw.'

The old man opened one eye. 'Walpurgian?' he said in a cracked little voice. 'Did somebody say Walpurgian?'

Thomas and Melanie backed away. 'Are – are you a wizard?' Thomas asked cautiously.

'Wizard?' snapped the old man. 'Who says?'

'Well,' said Melanie, 'are you or aren't you?'

The old man thought for a moment. 'Depends who's asking,' he said cautiously. 'You i'n't witch-hunters, is you?'

''Course we're not,' said Thomas stoutly.

'No one hunts witches any more,' added Melanie. 'They used to, I know, they used to hunt them down and be cruel to them. But that was in olden days. People don't do that sort of thing any more.'

'So you're just a pair of Tiddler Britlanders?' asked the old man. Thomas nodded. 'Thank Walpurgis for that!' cried the old man, scrambling to his feet, and making an elaborate bow to Melanie, like the pictures of Sir Walter Raleigh bowing to Queen Elizabeth the First.

'Hieronymus Tosh, Esquire,' he announced grandly,

'your humbly devoted Magikerry-Trickery Man, Ma'am.'

Melanie held out her hand, and the old man kissed it. 'Miss Melanie Brace-Girdle,' she announced.

Thomas, not to be outdone, made a deep bow. 'Master Thomas Grey,' he said.

They took old Hieronymus Tosh across the clearing to the tree-house. 'My, my, that's very fine, that is,' said the old man, gazing up into the branches.

'It's a tree-house,' said Thomas.

'I can see that,' mumbled the old man. 'I may be old, Tiddler Britlander, but old Hieronymus i'n't stupid.'

Mr Majeika was standing at the foot of the tree in his pyjamas and dressing-gown, looking out anxiously for the children.

'And that's our teacher,' said Melanie.

'He's from Walpurgis, too,' said Thomas.

'He i'n't, is he?' The old man was astonished.

'He is,' said Thomas.

'Guess what!' Melanie called to Mr Majeika. 'We've found another wizard in the woods!'

Mr Majeika's eyes opened wide. Slowly, he approached Hieronymus Tosh. Slowly, old Tosh approached Mr Majeika. They eyed each other like two cats wondering whether to fight. Then, slowly, each smiled at the other.

'Hail, Walpurgis!' chanted Mr Majeika.

'Hail, Walpurgis!' chanted Hieronymus Tosh.

Each of them bowed three times to the other. Then they both stood on one leg and shook hands under the other leg, winding their free arms round the backs of their necks. Then they repeated this curious handshake using the other leg and the other arm. Finally, they pulled each other's nose three times.

116

'Wow!' said Thomas. 'I think we've just seen a real Walpurgian greeting.'

In the tree-house, they served Hieronymus Tosh the remaining fish fingers, followed by an orange from the fruitbowl that Mr Majeika had conjured up. The old man ate the orange in a curious fashion, throwing away all the inside part and eating the peel.

'How long have you been in Britland, Wizard Tosh?' asked Mr Majeika, as the old man finished his meal.

'I i'n't so sure,' said Hieronymus Tosh, considering the matter carefully. 'Quite a few days now, that's for certain. But I i'n't much good at figures.'

'What brought you here?' said Melanie.

'Were you banished, like Mr Majeika?' asked Thomas.

'Thomas!' said Mr Majeika reprovingly.

But the old man did not seem to mind. 'Banished? Me? Good Galaxies, no! I applied for Overseas Service. They gave me an aptitude test, and it showed me to be "Bombastic and Boring", so they said I'd make an ideal teacher.' He munched some more orange peel.

'Where did they send you in Britland?' asked Mr Majeika.

'Little place called Much Barty,' said the old man, munching. 'Ever been there?'

The children looked at each other in amazement.

'Well, if you i'n't, then you i'n't missed much,' said the old man.

'What did you teach?' asked Mr Majeika.

The old man thought carefully for a long time. 'Children,' he said.

'What Mr Majeika means,' said Thomas, 'is, did you teach things like Maths? You know, numbers?'

Hieronymus Tosh shook his head. 'No, no, far too difficult.'

'Writing?' asked Melanie.

The old man shook his head again. 'No time for that.' He thought hard. 'It might've been . . .'

'Yes?' asked Thomas.

'Tapestry,' said Hieronymus Tosh. 'And mebbe a little Jousting too.'

'Tapestry and Jousting?' Melanie repeated. 'Were you very good at them?'

'No good at all,' said the old man. 'You don't have to be good at anything to be a teacher, do you, eh, Wizard? You just have to be able to put up with Tiddlers, with Bratlings.' He grinned at Mr Majeika, who grinned back.

'So how long were you a teacher?' asked Mr Majeika.

'Oh, a long time,' said old Tosh. 'About a week.'

'A week?' said Melanie indignantly. 'You call that long?'

'That's all I could stand. Weren't no fun, it weren't.'

'And then?' asked Thomas.

'Then,' said the old man dreamily, 'then I ran away.'

'That's not very brave,' said Melanie.

'No,' said Hieronymus Tosh, 'but it were downright sensible.'

'When exactly did you run away?' Mr Majeika wondered.

'I can tell you that,' answered Tosh. 'I can place it exac'ly. 'Twas the day before that jolly tar Columbus discovered Ameriky.'

'Cor!' said Thomas. 'That was in 1492. You've been here . . .' he did some quick arithmetic on his fingers '. . . nearly five hundred years!'

'Had a feeling it was quite a while,' said Hieronymus Tosh.

They made the old man a cup of herbal tea (it was the

sort of thing he had been drinking in the woods for five hundred years) and they lit the oil lamp, while he told them more of his strange experiences.

'What have you been doing since you gave up teaching and ran away?' asked Mr Majeika.

'Doing?' grunted the old man. 'Why, keeping out o' the way o' witch-hunters, of course.'

A frown crossed Mr Majeika's face. 'Witch-hunters?' he asked. 'What are witch-hunters?'

'You mean you i'n't heard?' The old man was astonished. 'In Britland, if they suspect a person is a wizard, or a witch, why, the poor feller or woman gets tied to a ducking stool.'

Mr Majeika's eyes opened wide. 'And then?' he asked anxiously.

'They gets thrown,' pronounced Hieronymus Tosh gloomily, 'into a deep pool.'

'Oh!' said Mr Majeika, looking thoroughly frightened. An awful vision crossed his brain of Hamish Bigmore, dressed as a medieval witch-hunter, tying him to a stool and plunging him into the depths of the Much Barty duck pond.

'Couldn't you swim out again?' he asked the old man anxiously.

'No hope,' answered Hieronymus Tosh. 'They tied up your arms and legs with rope. And if you happened to float to the surface, and not drown, that proved you had magical powers, so they bumped you off some other way.'

'Oh!' said Mr Majeika faintly.

'And if you did drown, well, that proved you weren't a wizard.'

'It was a bit late then!' whimpered Mr Majeika.

'Exactly,' said Hieronymus Tosh gloomily. 'So, not fancying any of that, I took off to these woods.'

'What other nasty things did they do to witches and wizards?' asked Thomas interestedly.

'That's enough of that, Thomas,' announced Mr Majeika briskly. 'Time for bed.'

Mr Majeika waited until the children were asleep before he whispered to Hieronymus Tosh: 'Why ever don't you try to get back to Walpurgis?'

The old man, who was rocking in Mr Majeika's hammock, answered impatiently: ''Course I tried. I tried plenty of times. Old Hieronymus i'n't stupid, you know. Tried all I could, I did. All kinds o' spells, incantations, conjurations . . . But it weren't no use.'

'Why not?' asked Mr Majeika, anxious that the same thing might happen when he wanted to get back to Walpurgis.

'Because,' the old man said crossly, 'when I left, when I came down 'ere, some daft meddling wizard up there classified me as *Missing Without Trace*.'

'Oh!' said Mr Majeika, aghast.

'So here I am,' continued Hieronymus Tosh. 'A wizard lost in the midst of time, Mr Majeika.'

And with that, he fell fast asleep, leaving a very worried Mr Majeika to sit up all night wondering how he could help the old man – and wondering if he too were stuck in Britland for ever, whether in five hundred years' time some children, out gathering sticks, might find him living a bare existence in the woods of Bartyshire.

He was still awake at dawn. Restlessly, he wandered out on to the balcony of the tree-house. After a few minutes' thought, he gazed up into the skies. It was weeks now since the Worshipful Wizard had spoken in his ear. If Walpurgis didn't call him, how could he call them? (He didn't know about Wilhelmina's upside-down long-distance phone calls, and anyway there was no telephone in the tree-house.)

He lifted his head to the sky, and shouted up through the branches of the tree: 'Hello, Walpurgis! Majeika calling! Are you receiving me? Hello, Walpurgis! Majeika calling! Are you receiving me? Come in, Walpurgis!'

There was a long pause, and then suddenly a voice in his ear said crossly: *'Don't you know what time it is, Majeika? Can't it wait till morning? We're all fast asleep up here.'*

'You're always all asleep up there, sir,' muttered Mr Majeika, remembering the sleeping wizards who had endlessly failed him in his 'O'-Levels.

'What's that, Majeika?'

'Oh, nothing, sir,' said Mr Majeika hastily. 'Listen, sir. I've got some good news. I've found a lost wizard.'

'A what, Majeika?'

'A long-lost wizard, sir. He was sent to Much Barty in the year 1492, to teach Tapestry and Jousting.'

'Tosh!' said the Worshipful Wizard, still cross at being woken.

'That's *it*, sir! Tosh! Hieronymus Tosh.'

'Hm.' The Worshipful Wizard was thinking. *'Wait a minute, I've got the Register of Missing Necromancers here, let's have a look.'* There was a pause while he turned the pages. *'Hm, Wizard Bottles lost in the Bermuda Triangle . . . Wizard Gateau lost in the Black Forest . . . Ah yes, Wizard Tosh, Exit Visa from Walpurgis granted the day before they discovered America. Well, what about it?'*

'Well, sir, he's here. And he wants to go back to Walpurgis.'

'Hm, well, we don't normally open the border for re-entry until after breakfast, but I suppose in this case . . . Five hundred years and all that . . .'

'Oh, thank you, sir!' said Mr Majeika delightedly. 'I'll fetch him right away.'

121

He dragged old Hieronymus Tosh out of bed, and explained everything to him.

'*Welcome back to the fold, Hieronymus*,' said the Worshipful Wizard as Tosh came out on to the balcony.

'Thank you, sir,' answered the old man. 'I've been waiting for this moment for five hundred years, sir.'

He and Mr Majeika gave a Walpurgian bear-hug, and wished each other farewell.

'*Ready for re-entry, Tosh?*'

'Oh yes, sir. Thank you, Wizard Majeika, and goodbye!'

'Safe journey, Wizard Hieronymus!' called Mr Majeika, and with a flash and a puff of smoke the old man was gone.

The noise woke Thomas and Melanie, and they hurried to the tree-house door.

'Does that mean he's gone back to Walpurgis?' they asked.

Mr Majeika nodded. 'And it's time for us to go, too,' he said. 'Back to Camp.'

The children groaned, but there was no changing his mind. They climbed down the ladder and took one last look at the tree-house. Mr Majeika's hair began to wiggle.

'Oh, Mr Majeika, do you *have* to?' Thomas asked sadly.

'Afraid so, Thomas,' he answered, as the tree-house began to vanish before their eyes.

'But why?' asked Melanie.

'You should know the answer,' laughed Mr Majeika. 'It's magical, Melanie!'

Five minutes later they were back at the Camp. Everyone was getting dressed and making breakfast. 'Ah, Majeika!' said Mr Potter. 'Been for a spell in the woods?'

'You could say that,' Mr Majeika replied.

Everyone helped to strike camp and pack the tents and the sleeping-bags on to their bicycles. 'I thought,' said Mr Potter, 'that on the way back we might stop off for a moment to take a look at an historic feature of Much Barty. A local monument, you might call it.'

'That sounds interesting,' said Mr Majeika.

But when he got there, he found it thoroughly frightening: it was the Much Barty Ducking Stool, preserved from medieval days when the folk of Much Barty tied Witches and Wizards to it and ducked them in the village pond.

The Ducking Stool was still working, and they gave a demonstration of it to Mr Majeika – though without anyone tied to it. 'In! Out! In! Out!' shouted Hamish Bigmore, as the stool was raised and lowered into the water.

'They used them for testing Wizards, don't you know,' Mr Potter explained to Mr Majeika. 'Not the sort of thing we'd go in for today, eh?'

'No,' said Mr Majeika, wiping his brow. 'No, indeed.'

6

BREAKING UP
IS HARD TO DO

'*So you've finally reached the last day of term, Majeika?*' said the voice of the Worshipful Wizard in Mr Majeika's ear, early one morning.

'Indeed I have, sir.' Mr Majeika contemplated his calendar. 'July 41st,' it read. It was a Walpurgian calendar. Mr Majeika knew the dates were a bit different down here in Britland, but the Walpurgian calendar reminded him of home.

'*Time to come back to Walpurgis, would you say, Majeika?*' asked the Worshipful Wizard, who might have been reading Mr Majeika's thoughts.

'And resume my Sorcery studies, sir?' said Mr Majeika, thrilled to bits. 'Oh, sir, I can't wait! Can I set off tomorrow?' He rushed over to his desk and began to stuff all his books and papers into his satchel.

'*In rather a hurry, aren't you, Majeika?*' remarked the Worshipful Wizard. '*Remember, it will mean entirely giving up the noble art of teaching.*'

'Oh, I don't mind that, sir. I can think of nothing better than giving up teaching Hamish Bigmore.'

'*Hm, maybe. But I thought you had taken quite a liking to one or two of the Britland bratlings, Majeika. The Tiddlers, as our friend Hieronymus Tosh is wont to call them.*'

Mr Majeika thought for a moment. 'Well, yes, sir, I

have. But perhaps I wouldn't have to say goodbye to them for ever, sir. Perhaps they could come up and visit me in Walpurgis sometimes?'

There was a snort from the Worshipful Wizard. *'Don't talk nonsense, Majeika. You know no Britlander has ever set foot in Walpurgis, nor ever will.'*

'No, sir, I suppose not, sir. Well, that does make it all rather difficult, sir. I'll have to think about it. But I do want to try those exams again, sir.'

Thomas Grey turned up early for the last day of school. He didn't want to miss the last lessons with Mr Majeika.

'Good morning, Thomas,' said Mr Potter. 'Looking forward to breaking up?'

'Not really, sir,' said Thomas. 'I mean, school's a lot more fun these days, sir.'

They watched as Mr Majeika arrived on his tricycle, which as usual was rather out of control. Papers were tumbling out of his satchel and scattering to the wind. Several of Class Three, including Melanie, were running alongside, laughing and cheering.

'Yes,' said Mr Potter. 'It is, isn't it?'

'So,' said the Worshipful Wizard to his colleagues, in the Wizards' Chamber up in Walpurgis, 'he wants to come home. At least I think he does, and really it's about time he did. He's been a pretty good teacher, and I think he's had about enough punishment for failing his exams. So, all those in favour of allowing Apprentice Wizard Majeika back again?'

Almost all the Wizards were asleep. No one raised a hand.

'Not much enthusiasm there,' the Worshipful Wizard

observed. 'Still, I don't imagine there are any objections, are there? Nobody against?'

Someone cleared his throat. The Worshipful Wizard blinked and looked along the line of sleeping sorcerers. One person *was* awake. Very wide awake, in fact: a severe-looking gentleman with a pointed beard and sharp eyes. A label in front of his seat stated: 'Chief Examiner: Wizard Marks.'

'Any objections, Marks?' asked the Worshipful Wizard.

'Just a small point of order, Your Worshipfulness.'

'Ah,' said the Worshipful Wizard. 'What is it?'

'Despite the best will in the world,' snapped Wizard Marks, 'Apprentice Wizard Majeika cannot be processed back into Walpurgis until the neccessary documentation re Re-Registration has been signed by me, sir, in tetra-triplicate.'

'Ah,' said the Worshipful Wizard again. 'It was you, Marks, as I recall, who constantly failed Majeika in his exams.'

'Yes, sir,' said Wizard Marks. 'It's my job, sir. My post as Chief Examiner, Wizards.'

'Quite so,' said the Worshipful Wizard, who did not in the least care for Wizard Marks, an interfering point-of-order sort of fellow who was always telling you that your shoelaces were tied up wrong and unimportant things of that kind. 'Well,' said the Worshipful Wizard, 'can you get on with this – whatever it is – Re-Registration in triplicate, and all that stuff? It won't take long, will it?'

Wizard Marks smiled a rather unpleasant smile. 'We can't proceed quite so fast, sir. Regulations require a final check.'

'Check?'

'On his conduct, sir. Just to make sure he really is behaving himself among the Britlanders, sir. After all, Paragraph 920, Sub-Section 4,003 in the *Good Wizard*

126

Guide does state quite clearly that no Britlander-based Wizard shall be allowed to return to Walpurgis should he be caught in Britland doing *anything Walpurgian.*'

'Ah,' the Worshipful Wizard said, uncomfortably recalling that he had granted Mr Majeika unofficial permission to do several thoroughly Walpurgian things when faced with Wilhelmina Worlock. 'Well, in that case you'd better . . .'

'Check, sir? It'll be my pleasure.'

And snapping shut a folder labelled *Report on Apprentice Wizard Majeika*, Wizard Marks sharpened several pencils and set off for Britland.

'What do you mean, you may not be here next term, Mr Majeika?' Mr Potter said aghast, staring at Class Three's teacher across a pile of end-of-term reports. 'You can't do this to us! We need you!'

'It's very difficult to explain, Mr Potter,' Mr Majeika sighed. 'Let's just say I'm waiting for –' and he pointed a finger in the air '– the Call.'

'Good gracious! I didn't know you were the religious type. But in any case your calling is here, Majeika. We all depend utterly on you to keep Hamish – er, Class Three in order. It could be months, years, before I find anyone else with your skills. You just can't do this to us!'

'I'm sorry, Mr Potter,' Mr Majeika said meekly. 'It's simply that I am in the hands of Higher Powers.'

One of those Higher Powers was closer at hand than Mr Majeika realized. Wizard Marks descended swiftly from Walpurgis, using his umbrella as a parachute, and landed on the edge of the Much Barty village green, where a Ladies' Cricket Match was in progress.

Councillor Mrs Brace-Girdle hit the ball for six just as Wizard Marks touched down. He was wearing a bowler hat and pin-striped trousers, and was carrying a briefcase. The ball flew through the air and hit his bowler hat. Walpurgian hats are as hard as concrete, and the ball split in two.

The cricketing ladies stared in amazement, but Wizard Marks paid no attention. Another ball was found, and the match resumed.

Wizard Marks was aware that several white-flannelled Britlanders were playing some children's game or other, but his mission was far too important for him to pay attention to such trifles. He set off for the school, which lay straight across the village green, so Wizard Marks strode slap through the middle of the cricketers, just as Mrs Brace-Girdle hit the ball another mighty stroke. It zoomed straight at him, but he coolly held out his umbrella and impaled the ball on its point.

Wizard Marks strode past the open-mouthed ladies in silence.

At last Mrs Brace-Girdle found her tongue. 'I say!' she called out. 'Please can we have our ball back?'

'Now, Majeika,' said Mr Potter at break-time, 'you haven't forgotten what day it is today, have you?'

'End of term, Mr Potter,' said Mr Majeika brightly.

'And what do we do at the end of term at St Barty's?' Mr Potter asked.

Mr Majeika thought for a moment. 'Go home?' he suggested.

'Yes, Majeika, but before that? Evidently you are unaware of an ancient tradition at St Barty's. On the last day of the summer term, Majeika, we commemorate the founding of this noble seat of learning by my ancestor, the

Reverend Sir Bartholomew Potter, Vicar of Much Barty many generations ago, who thus ensured that all future generations of Potters should have the, hrrm, great pleasure of teaching here. And do you know how we commemorate it, Majeika?'

Mr Majeika shook his head.

'We take out a special bust of our Founder, Majeika, a statue. And then what do you suppose we do to it?'

'Er, set fire to it, Mr Potter?' guessed Mr Majeika. The ways of these Britlanders were still a great puzzle to him.

'No, Majeika, we unveil it. In the course of a very special ceremony at which one of our youngsters plays the role of the Eternal Pupil. All very ceremonial, don't you know?'

'A real Britlander ceremony, Mr Potter! Oh, I've always wanted to go to one.'

'And here, Majeika, is my costume for the ceremony. Perhaps you'd help me on with it.'

Mr Majeika looked at the strange garment Mr Potter was attempting to put on. 'A sheet, Mr Potter?'

'This isn't a sheet, Majeika. Where were you educated? This is a Roman toga, symbol of a classical education, token of the great learning that goes on here at St Barty's. All the children will be wearing them. Remember, Majeika, all education is founded upon a study of the Classics. So, Majeika, let us commence preparations for this afternoon's great event. And first of all, Majeika, *Bustium ad Plinthium.*'

'I beg your pardon, Mr Potter? I'm afraid I don't speak Chinese.'

'Chinese, Majeika? This is Latin, Majeika, Latin! Much of today's ceremony will be conducted in it. *Bustium ad Plinthium* – meaning, put the bust on the plinth.'

'The bust on the –'

'Plinth, Majeika, plinth. In plainer English, that stone object standing in the middle of the garden. You'll find the bust of Sir Bartholomew in my study, on the top shelf of the Trophy Cupboard. Hurry along now, Majeika. I want everything spick and span by the time the Governors arrive at two o'clock.'

'Yes, Mr Potter.'

'And see that Sir Bartholomew is well dusted and polished.'

'Just as you say, Mr Potter.' And Mr Majeika, more puzzled than ever by the strange habits of the Britlanders, trotted off to Mr Potter's study.

Wizard Marks reached the gateway of the school, but he did not come up the drive. He lingered at the railings, briefcase in hand. Considering the matter for a moment, he decided to occupy a vantage point, under a large tree, which would allow him to see without being easily seen. There was a stone object placed on the lawn, he noted, and several chairs set out in a row. It appeared that a religious festival was about to take place. Probably Majeika would be taking part in it. There was as good a chance here as anywhere of spotting the silly fellow getting up to something Walpurgian.

Wizard Marks took out his Report form and a sharp pencil, and waited.

Mr Majeika found the Trophy Cupboard in a corner of Mr Potter's study, and eventually discovered the bust of Sir Bartholomew under a pile of old cricket stumps, footballs, and other school odds and ends. 'The old codger certainly does look a bit like Mr Potter,' he mused to himself, as he gave the top of its head a polish with his sleeve. 'But there's not much of him, just the head and shoulders. Poor Sir Bartholomew! Whatever happened to the rest of you?'

'Cor, you *do* look silly in your togas,' Hamish Bigmore smirked at Thomas and Melanie.

'Not half as silly as you,' snorted Thomas. 'The Eternal Pupil! Cor, you *will* make a fool of yourself laying that wreath on the bust.'

'Mr Potter has chosen *me* for a very important task,' Hamish said grandly. 'Not like you two. You're just a couple of Roman slaves, lifting a silly old cloth off the statue. Anyway, where *is* the silly old statue?' he continued, looking at the empty plinth.

'Mr Majeika's just gone to fetch it,' said Melanie.

'Oh,' said Hamish Bigmore thoughtfully. 'Has he?'

'Come along then, Sir Bartholomew,' muttered Mr Majeika as he manhandled the heavy bust out of Mr Potter's study and down the passage towards the garden. 'Soon have you *ad plinthium*, as they say in Chinese – I mean, in Latin. Carefully does it . . .'

And down the steps he teetered, into the garden.

'Afternoon, Mr Majeika, *sir*,' said the mocking voice of Hamish Bigmore. And out stuck Hamish Bigmore's foot; and the bust of Sir Bartholomew nearly went flying.

Nearly, but not quite. Hamish ran off, grinning to himself, quite certain he had caused a disaster. But Mr Majeika managed to hang on to the bust, regain his balance, and stagger off down the path with it still safely in his arms. 'That was a near thing, Sir Bartholomew!' he muttered. 'I'll get even with that Hamish. But you're safe now, Sir Bartholomew.'

At which point Mr Majeika tripped over a stone step.

*

131

'Come along, Hamish!' Mr Potter called, waving the laurel wreath that Hamish, as the Eternal Pupil, was supposed to carry. 'We must have a quick rehearsal before the Governors arrive. Where have you been?'

'Sorry, Mr Potter,' smirked Hamish. 'I've just been having a little, er, bust-up.'

Thomas and Melanie exchanged glances. 'Where is the bust, sir?' Melanie asked Mr Potter.

'Where is it, indeed?' repeated Mr Potter. 'Can't think what's keeping Majeika.'

Thomas and Melanie came round the corner from the lawn and found him desperately trying to mend the bust.

'It was just a little accident, Sir Bartholomew,' whimpered Mr Majeika over the broken pieces. 'Please, Sir Bartholomew, do stick yourself together again, even if I can't remember the Walpurgian spell to mend you. There, I think that's done it,' he went on, putting the pieces back together again. 'Now all we need is some glue. I'll take it to the kitchen and find some.'

But when he picked up the pieces, the whole thing fell apart again, breaking into small fragments on the gravel.

'He's really done it now!' said Thomas. 'What on earth is going to happen?'

'Melanie! Thomas! Come along!' called Mr Potter's voice. 'The Governors are arriving.'

'Oh, cripes!' said Mr Majeika. 'Oh, cripes!'

Mr Potter was welcoming the Governors at the gate of the school. Their Chairman, Councillor Mrs Brace-Girdle, had hurried over from her Ladies' Cricket Match without having had time to change out of her cricketing

132

gear. 'How good of you all to come,' smiled Mr Potter at them. 'And Bunty! How smart you look in your pads.'

The Governors took their seats in the garden, opposite the plinth, over which a white cloth had been draped.

'The bust of Sir Bartholomew is ready to be unveiled once more,' Mr Potter explained to them. 'Our new teacher, Majeika, has cleaned it up specially.'

'Has he,' snorted Mrs Brace-Girdle. 'I wonder if he had anything to do with that strange fellow who came marching straight through our cricket match just now, and speared the ball on the end of his umbrella. I bet Majeika's behind it. All the peculiar happenings in Much Barty these last few weeks can be traced back to him.'

Wizard Marks, hiding behind his tree, lifted an eyebrow, and made a hurried note on his Report form.

'Now, children!' called Mr Potter. 'In you all come. *Pueri et Puellae ad Plinthium.* Boys and girls to the plinth!'

In trooped Class Three in their togas, each of them wearing a small laurel wreath as a crown. 'What's going to happen about the bust of Sir Bartholomew?' Melanie whispered to Thomas.

'I don't know,' said Thomas. 'We'll find out the worst when we unveil it.'

'There's *something* up there on the plinth,' whispered Melanie. 'Do you think he's found another bust, or has he managed to mend Sir Bartholomew after all?'

'We'll find out soon enough when we unveil it,' whispered Thomas. 'Ssh, Mr Potter's beginning his speech.'

Hitching up his toga and adjusting his spectacles, Mr Potter took his place before the plinth. 'Friends, Governors, Bartyans,' he began in a sing-song voice, 'we are gathered here today to honour the memory of one of our old indestructibles. I refer, of course, to Sir Bartholomew Potter, of hallowed memory. Sir Bartholomew Potter, whose bust everlasting reminds us all of ... of ...' (as usual, Mr Potter had lost his place) '. . . of what a piece of work is man, how noble in reason, how infinite in . . . something else. And so let us see once more his visage of greatness. *Gaudeamus Igitur* – therefore let us rejoice! I give you all the Founder's Song!' And Mr Potter burst into mellifluous melody:

> 'O Founder Dear,
> We're gathered here
>> In memory of your name.
> Our children now
> Will scrape and bow
>> In honour of your fame.'

Melanie and Thomas walked, as they had been instructed, up to the plinth and took the edges of the cloth which was covering the place where the bust was supposed to be.

'And now,' continued Mr Potter, 'movingly, they lift the cloth, kindly lent to us as always by the Cherry Tree Tea Rooms, to reveal – our Founder!'

'Here goes,' whispered Melanie, and together they removed the cloth.

'It's Sir Bartholomew all right,' whispered Thomas, looking with relief at the white alabaster bust on the plinth before them. 'He must have mended it.'

'No it's not!' whispered Melanie. '*It's Mr Majeika!*'

And the bust gave them a wink.

By the railings, Wizard Marks was looking on in a bored fashion at the ceremony. Such trivial nonsense these Britlanders engaged in! He was wasting his time down here with them. And no sign of Majeika anywhere. No sign at all . . .

'Wait a minute,' thought Wizard Marks, 'there's something familiar about that bust.'

*

'He's magical, Melanie!' whispered Thomas. 'How did he do it?'

'He's simply magicked himself into being the bust!' Melanie whispered back. 'It's the cleverest thing he's ever done. And it looks exactly like Sir Bartholomew, unless you peer too closely.'

'That's marvellous,' whispered Thomas. 'He'll get away with breaking the real bust.'

'Watch out,' said Melanie under her breath. 'Here comes Hamish Bigmore. Let's hope he doesn't spot anything.'

'And now,' Mr Potter was saying, 'I call upon the Eternal Pupil, *Bigmorus Minimus* . . .'

''S'me, now, Mummy!' Hamish interrupted, waving at Pam Bigmore. 'Look, Mummy, 's'me!'

'. . . the Eternal Pupil, *Bigmorus Minimus*, who will honour the Founder with his Wreath of Learning.'

Hamish advanced slowly with the wreath. He mounted the steps of the plinth, and came face to face with the bust. He paused for an instant, and stared.

'He's recognized Mr Majeika!' whispered Melanie.

'But he won't dare do anything,' whispered Thomas.

Hamish seemed frozen as he looked in amazement at the bust. He opened his mouth to say something. Then he evidently thought better of it, lifted his wreath, and rammed it down over the shoulders of 'Sir Bartholomew'.

'O Founder, we salute thee! *Salute Magister!*' called Mr Potter.

'*Salute Magister!*' answered Class Three, and bowed to the bust.

Up on the plinth, Mr Majeika had a problem. Hamish Bigmore had put the wreath over him so that one of the leaves was tickling his nose. He was going to sneeze.

Thomas and Melanie, watching him intently, spotted

the trouble. Climbing up to the top step, they moved the wreath before it was too late, and each of them held a finger over the nose of the 'bust' to stop the sneeze.

'Thank you!' mouthed the bust.

'*Salute Magister!*' cried Mr Potter again. 'Well done, children, you may all go now. And ladies and gentlemen,' he said, turning to the Governors, 'do come into my study for tea and cucumber sandwiches. Such a ceremony! Unbelievably moving, as always, wasn't it?' And dabbing away a tear, Mr Potter led his guests indoors.

Class Three ran off – all except Melanie and Thomas, who lingered in the shrubbery to see what would happen next.

And from the railings, Wizard Marks was watching as well.

No sooner had Class Three gone than Hamish Bigmore came tiptoeing back. He mounted the steps to the plinth, looked cautiously around him, decided that he was unobserved by anyone, and drew back his right arm.

'He's going to punch Mr Majeika on the nose!' whispered Thomas.

'Ouch!' came a cry – but not from Mr Majeika. Hamish had let fly a punch, but the 'bust', for that moment at least, *was* made of stone. Off went Hamish, nursing a very sore hand.

And a few moments later, off went Mr Majeika. The plinth suddenly began to move, and Thomas and Melanie could see a pair of feet sticking out from beneath it.

'So he was just standing inside it,' said Thomas.

Melanie shook her head. 'There was more to it than that. When Hamish hit him, he was as hard as stone. It was definitely magical, Thomas!'

Wizard Marks, writing on his Report, was of the same opinion.

*

Melanie and Thomas were on their way back into the school building when they saw Hamish trotting past with a cardboard box full of bits and pieces. 'Do you know what he had in there?' Thomas asked when Hamish had gone.

'No idea,' said Melanie.

'The remains of the bust. The real one. What do you think he's up to?'

'Dunno. We'd better follow him and find out.'

Hamish was on his way down the passage to Mr Potter's study, where the Governors were having their tea-party. He knocked at the door.

'Who is it?' sang out Mr Potter's voice from within.

'*Bigmorus Minimus*, sir. Oh, Mr Potter, sir. I've got something to show you.'

'Not your usual nose-bleed, Hamish? Don't waste my time, boy, I've got the Governors in here.'

'No sir, something much more exciting than a nose-bleed. It's –'

Two pairs of hands, Thomas's and Melanie's, shot out and covered Hamish Bigmore's mouth. 'You're coming with us, *Bigmorus Minimus*,' hissed Thomas.

'And so you see, Mr Majeika, he was going to tell on you to Mr Potter, and in front of the Governors, too.'

Mr Majeika sighed. 'You're rather fond of telling tales, Hamish, aren't you?'

'What, sir? Me, sir? Not me, sir. I was just doing a spot of tidying up, sir, and I found these bits, sir, and I was going to ask Mr Potter what to do with them ...' He tried to wriggle free from the grip in which Thomas and Melanie still held him.

'Liar! Liar! Pants on fire!' chanted Thomas.

'You deserve a good box round the ears from your Mummy,' remarked Melanie.

Mr Majeika was scratching his head. 'I really don't know what to do about you, Hamish. What's that you said, Melanie? "Box round the ears"? Is that a Britland punishment?'

Melanie nodded.

'It sounds rather an odd idea, but if you think it might work . . .' And Mr Majeika's hair began to twitch.

Pam Bigmore and her husband Ronnie Bigmore were both at the school gate with the white Rolls-Royce, number-plate B I G 1, to collect Hamish at four o'clock.

For a change, Hamish Bigmore was the last to come out of school.

'Well, well, darling,' said Pam when she saw him. 'You *have* been having some fun today, I can tell that.'

Ronnie Bigmore stared at his son. ''E's got a cardboard box on 'is head,' he said slowly.

'I can see that, Ronnie. And Mummy knows why, Hamish. It's called "creative play". *I* know why you've got a cardboard box on your head, little Hamish, it's because you're a very imaginative boy, and you like playing funny games all by yourself. You live in a little world of your own, don't you, Hamish? Yes you do! And who's having a nice little adventure in there right now, eh, Hamish?' And she patted the cardboard box indulgently. 'Come along, Hamish, let's go off to the Cherry Tree Tea Rooms and give you a lovely cream tea, and Hamish, you can keep that funny old cardboard box on your head just as long as you jolly well like! Aren't you a clever, creative little boy? Oh look, Ronnie, he's pretending he can't get it off his head!'

'It wasn't meant to be that sort of box,' Melanie explained

to Mr Majeika. '"Box round the ears" means hitting someone, with your fists.'

'Oh dear,' said Mr Majeika.

'And what's Hamish going to do?' asked Thomas. 'Did you mean him not to be able to get the box off again?'

'Not really,' Mr Majeika said sheepishly. 'It was rather a strong spell, I admit. But I expect it will wear off in half an hour or so.'

'But it's already half an hour since you magicked the box on to him,' said Melanie. 'And he still can't get it off.'

'Well,' said Mr Majeika, 'maybe a Walpurgian half-hour.'

'How long is that?' asked Thomas.

'About twenty-four Britland hours,' said Mr Majeika. 'By the way, I've got some news for you. They've sent my Exit Visa down from Walpurgis. It came at lunchtime, by special delivery.' He held up a glittering envelope.

'Exit Visa?' asked Melanie. 'What does that mean?'

'It means,' said Mr Majeika, 'that I'm going back to Walpurgis.'

Thomas and Melanie looked blankly at each other.

'But you *can't*!' they both said at once.

'Oh yes I can,' said Mr Majeika cheerily. 'I need to get on with my Sorcery Studies. I'm sure they'll find a nice replacement teacher for you and the rest of Class Three. Now don't get upset, let's go off to the Cherry Tree Tea Rooms and celebrate the end of term. Oh, please cheer up or you'll make me miserable too.'

Wizard Marks completed his Report and set off on his return journey to Walpurgis, using his umbrella as a rocket. Nobody saw him go.

*

'Yes, Mrs Brace-Girdle,' said Mr Potter, 'we've definitely got to find a replacement teacher for Class Three. Such a pity, when Majeika was getting on so well, but there you are. He seems to have had a *call* to go into the Church, if I understand him aright, and one cannot stand in the way of Higher Things, eh, dear lady?'

'Mr Majeika a Vicar!' remarked Councillor Mrs Brace-Girdle, astounded. 'Whatever next! Still, Mr Potter, I can't disguise my delight in seeing the last of him as a teacher. You say you haven't yet found a replacement?'

'No indeed. There are plenty of advertisements in the *Times Educational Supplement* placed by teachers seeking posts in schools such as ours, but – for some reason – each of them contains the words: "Anything considered but Much Barty." It seems that our, er, reputation is spreading.'

'You know, Mr Potter,' said Mrs Brace-Girdle thoughtfully, 'I myself have often felt a calling for the educational profession.'

'You, Mrs Brace-Girdle?'

'Indeed yes. Of course, any teaching would have to fit in with all my Committees, but I think I could manage it. Would you consider taking me on?'

Mr Potter dimpled at her. 'Nothing, my dear Bunty, would give me greater pleasure. And I'm sure Class Three will be absolutely delighted.'

'Guess what,' said Melanie to Thomas. 'Well, no, you'd never guess, not in a month of Sundays. I thought there could be nothing worse than Mr Majeika leaving. But there is. Mummy's going to teach Class Three.'

'Your mother?' said Thomas. 'Oh, cripes.'

Melanie looked at her watch. 'Come on,' she said. 'We ought to be getting over to the windmill, to say goodbye

140

to Mr Majeika. He said he was going at exactly seven o'clock, and it's nearly seven now. Hey, Thomas, what's the matter? You're not crying, are you?'

'Of course I'm not crying,' Thomas muttered, kicking a stone. 'But it's not *fair*. He's the bestest teacher we ever had, the bestest anyone could ever have in the whole wide world, and now he's going. And anyway, *you're* crying too.'

Mr Majeika was counting the minutes to seven o'clock, the time the Exit Visa had stated for his departure. He was looking forward immensely to going. Of course he was . . . So why did he have this funny feeling in the pit of his stomach, as if he didn't really want to go at all? And what was this dampness all round his eyes? He hadn't got a cold, so why was he snivelling?

'Mr Majeika! Mr Majeika! You can't go yet! You haven't said goodbye to us!' It was the voices of Thomas and Melanie, running up the path to the windmill.

Mr Majeika tried to call out, but he couldn't. Seven o'clock struck.

'*Majeika!*' said the voice of the Worshipful Wizard in his ear. '*It's time to go. Ready for Re-Entry.*'

'Th-thank you, sir, b-but . . .'

'*Yes, Majeika?*'

'B-but . . . I . . . I . . .'

'*Yes, Majeika?*'

'I d-don't want . . .'

'*Yes, Majeika? Get on with it.*'

Mr Majeika could hear the children getting near the windmill now. 'Mr Majeika! Mr Majeika!' they were calling.

And then in Mr Majeika's ears, another voice: '*This is Wizard Marks reporting to the Worshipful Wizard. Just got*

141

back from Britland, sir, and I'm afraid it's a clear case of Walpurgian methods being used without permission. To be specific, sir, an instance involving a statue, and another concerning a cardboard box. Most regrettable, and in the worst possible taste. I'm afraid I cannot possibly sign in tetra-triplicate, sir. Exit Visa for Majeika cancelled.'

There was a pause. Mr Majeika could hear the children running up the steps to the windmill.

'Did you hear that, Majeika?' asked the Worshipful Wizard.

'Yes, sir!' said Mr Majeika, smiling all over his face. 'Exit Visa cancelled!'

'It's back to school, then, Majeika.'

'You mean I'm stuck here, sir, with Class Three?'

'That's right, Majeika. Sorry about it, but rules are rules. Oh, and Majeika?'

'Yes, sir?'

'Try and behave yourself this time.'

'I will, sir, oh, I will!' Mr Majeika cried, and he ran out on to the steps of the windmill and gave Melanie and Thomas the biggest hug they had ever had in their lives.